PRIZE SURPRISE SWEEPSTAKES!

This month's prize:

A FABULOUS SHARP VIEWCAM!

This month, as a special surprise, we're giving away a Sharp ViewCam**, the big-screen camcorder that has revolutionized home videos!

This is the camcorder everyone's talking about! Sharp's new ViewCam has a big 3" full-color viewing screen with 180° swivel action that lets you control everything you record—and watch it at the same time! Features include a remote control (so you can get into the picture yourself), 8 power zoom, full-range auto focus, battery pack, recharger and more!

The next page contains two Entry Coupons (as does every book you received this shipment). Complete and return *all* the entry coupons; **the more times you enter, the better your chances of winning!**

Then keep your fingers crossed, because you'll find out by November 15, 1995 if you're the winner!

Remember: The more times you enter, the better your chances of winning!*

*NO PURCHASE OR OBLIGATION TO CONTINUE BEING A SUBSCRIBER NECESSARY TO ENTER. SEE THE BACK PAGE FOR ALTERNATE MEANS OF ENTRY, AND RULES.

**THE PROPRIETORS OF THE TRADEMARK ARE NOT ASSOCIATED WITH THIS PROMOTION.

PVC KAL

PRIZE SURPRISE
SWEEPSTAKES

OFFICIAL ENTRY COUPON

This entry must be received by: OCTOBER 30, 1995
This month's winner will be notified by: NOVEMBER 15, 1995

YES, I want to win the Sharp ViewCam! Please enter me in the drawing and let me know if I've won!

Name_____

Address_____ Apt._____

City   State/Prov.   Zip/Postal Code

Account #_____

Return entry with invoice in reply envelope.

© 1995 HARLEQUIN ENTERPRISES LTD.   CVC KAL

PRIZE SURPRISE
SWEEPSTAKES

OFFICIAL ENTRY COUPON

This entry must be received by: OCTOBER 30, 1995
This month's winner will be notified by: NOVEMBER 15, 1995

YES, I want to win the Sharp ViewCam! Please enter me in the drawing and let me know if I've won!

Name_____

Address_____ Apt._____

City   State/Prov.   Zip/Postal Code

Account #_____

Return entry with invoice in reply envelope.

© 1995 HARLEQUIN ENTERPRISES LTD.   CVC KAL

Dear Reader,

Do you have a secret fantasy? Everybody does.
Maybe it's to be rich and famous and beautiful. Or to
start a no-strings affair with a sexy, mysterious stranger.
Or to have a sizzling second chance with a former
sweetheart.... You'll find these dreams—and much
more—in Temptation's exciting new yearlong
promotion, Secret Fantasies.

Mallory Rush continues to dazzle us with her
innovative and daring stories. We hope you had the
pleasure of reading *Love Game*—sexy at its best! (A
Harlequin release available in your bookstores now.) In
Kiss of the Beast, heroine Eva Campbell has a secret
fantasy. An expert on virtual reality, she's created the
perfect man on her computer. Except her fantasy lover
is much more real than she could ever imagine....

In the coming months, look for Secret Fantasies books
by JoAnn Ross and Glenda Sanders. Please write and
let us know how you enjoy the "fantasy."

Happy Reading!

The Editors
c/o Harlequin Temptation
225 Duncan Mill Road
Don Mills, Ontario
M3B 3K9
Canada

Dear Friends,

Secret Fantasies are just that—fantasies we secretly entertain. And secretly, I've always wondered what it would have been like for Beauty if the Beast had remained a beast.

Would she have loved him just as much? *No doubt.*

Would she have married him anyway? *You bet.*

And would they have lived happily ever after? *Surely so.*

But still, their lives would be different from that of a handsome prince and his bride. In *Kiss of the Beast* you'll meet one of my favorite heroes ever. Urich's quite a man, and yet he's not a man at all, he's—

Well...I can't really explain without giving part of the plot away, and I'm not about to spoil any surprises. But suffice it to say that this has to be the most unusual love story I've ever told. At the same time it is also the most fundamental. The primal struggle between man and woman, between our human and animal natures; the quest for self-acceptance and self-love; the search for a soul mate.

Beauty comes in many guises. And it is through a soul mate's eyes that beauty can be seen, even in a *Kiss of the Beast.*

Wishing you happily ever after,

Mallory Rush

Eva called out to him

An eternity of seconds passed and she frantically told herself she'd spoken too softly.

A subtle shift in the air raised the fine hair on the nape of her neck. Gooseflesh pricked her arms as a wisp of some formidable presence invaded her senses. Impossible. No one was here except her and her imagination.

Closing her eyes, she breathed deeply, inhaled what had to be an imaginary but nonetheless intoxicating scent—clean but earthy, it was purely animal and overwhelmingly male.

"Eva."

She opened her eyes and all she could do was stare. *He was here!* Moreover, her computer had certainly understood the definition of handsome. The ebony mane of his hair was brushed severely back, accentuating the exotic contours of his face. All angles and shadows, he radiated the savagery of a stalking wild beast.

As for his clothes...she really should have selected those. All black was fine, but they fit indecently well.

He grinned, revealing no lack of self-confidence. "Do you approve?"

"You're, uh...fine." She stumbled over her words, hardly able to take in what her eyes beheld. Her experiment had worked. And he was all hers....

Mallory Rush is a busy mother of five and author of twelve bestselling books, including two anthologies. She has also won the Career Achievement Award for Most Sensual Category Author from *Romantic Times* magazine. Mallory, who also writes as Olivia Rupprecht, lives in Wisconsin.

Books by Mallory Rush

HARLEQUIN TEMPTATION
448—LOVE SLAVE

HARLEQUIN BOOKS
LOVE GAME
OUTLAWS AND HEROES—"Danger and Desire"

Mallory Rush
KISS OF THE BEAST

Harlequin Books

TORONTO • NEW YORK • LONDON
AMSTERDAM • PARIS • SYDNEY • HAMBURG
STOCKHOLM • ATHENS • TOKYO • MILAN
MADRID • WARSAW • BUDAPEST • AUCKLAND

The most beautiful thing we can experience is the
mysterious. It is the source of all true art and science.
—Albert Einstein

ISBN 0-373-25658-2

KISS OF THE BEAST

Copyright © 1995 by Olivia Rupprecht.

Printed in U.S.A.

1

"SHE'S PERFECT for our purposes, Urich."

"There's no doubt of that in my mind, Raven," Urich said in fluent English, delicately flavored with the accent of his native tongue. "It won't be long before our nation is powerful again."

Urich focused on the woman they were spying upon from a room filled with equipment James Bond would die for. *To die for.* Such an odd vernacular these people used, but he'd mastered their English slang, devoted intense study of their customs. How better to disguise his true origins, than—how did they say it? Oh, yes. *When in Rome, do as the Romans do.* San Francisco, to be exact.

Watching her race toward the bland, concrete high-security building, Urich knew his skills would be challenged by their target for them.

Eva Campbell was that target. Tawny hair tumbling from a bun, she reached to shove back the pins and lost her hold on the bulging folder she was carrying.

Wind scattered the pages and she ran after them, the gusting air lifting her full skirt and exposing a generous length of pale thigh. A low vibration rose from Urich's throat, neck tendons taut as he strained closer to the surveillance screen for a better view.

"You're attracted," Raven, his fellow conspirator noted, heavy lines creasing his brow.

"Of course," Urich readily admitted. "But Raven, so are you." Urich knew Raven would save his breath from denying what was blatantly true. So it went when one could see into places of the mind where others couldn't go. Telepathy, some called it. Urich called it a gift wrapped in a curse, an ability he both damned and revered—just as he did those other "talents" that made him uniquely suited for this mission.

It was, by far, the most crucial, ambitious mission he'd ever undertaken. The future of their nation was riding on it. So was his reputation.

Perceiving his superior's concern over the attraction that could not, *would not*, interfere with his judgment, Urich said, "Never doubt my devotion to duty. Lest you forget, I am my father's son."

"I never forget that," Raven hastened to assure him, while his mental sigh of relief brought a thin smile to Urich's lips. "You should be leaving. Access is secured for your entry into her research room. Once you're there, it's up to you to convince her that you are who and what she believes you to be. Should suspicions be raised . . ."

"That would be most unfortunate," Urich said. "But don't worry. I'll make sure she's convinced."

"Good. It's much better for us—and Dr. Campbell—if she comes willingly instead of by less desirable means."

Urich gave a curt nod and prepared to assume his role. He would not fail. His skills would assist him considerably, but it was his extensive knowledge of the woman that would aid him the most.

Eva Campbell was a visionary scientist, a remarkable woman who saw as others did not. They had that in common, and much else. Fellow survivors from different worlds, they were prisoners of purpose, exiled by that which drove them.

It was his purpose to win her trust, coerce her with the powers he possessed. Eager for the challenge, and the victory he could already taste, Urich readied himself to slip into her life as if he were the man of her dreams.

Her dreams, he knew of those, too.

"OKAY, EVA, the chamber's ready. We're ready. We've *been* ready for the last hour. Come on, will you?"

"Let me check the master computer and the hologram bank one more time," she said anxiously. "And while I do that, double-check to make sure the camera's on and working."

"It's working, it's working already," Ethan assured her with an exasperated sigh.

He caught her scathing glance and pushed up the tortoiseshell glasses sliding down his nose. Eva was tempted to tweak it, just to remind him who was boss. The BoyWonder was a genius, for sure; but at twenty-four, a decade her junior, he had some growing up to do when it came to real life. Only it wasn't going to happen by spending all his time work, work, working with her.

Five years and she still thought of Ethan as a cute kid in a lab coat. A Doogie Howser brain and a Rick Moranis baby face—hey, if anyone could shrink the kids, Ethan was the physics expert most likely to succeed—he preferred working nights and weekends with her over dating some nice California girl.

That was no real surprise, either. His skater-cut hair and attempts to appear hip only seemed to emphasize the obvious: Ethan was basically a nerd. With braces.

"Yes?" she said testily when he tapped her shoulder.

"C'mon, Eva, enough."

"It's enough when I say it's enough," she growled.

"Chill out, would you? Pop a pill, zone out on Zen, whatever. Just quit acting so nervous."

"Of course, I'm nervous! And so are our funders. They want some results, and if this program screws up..." Eva

shuddered. Years of painstaking research and experimenta-
tion were at stake. Her life's work was a fantastical pipe
dream to the backers who had sanctioned the project but were
now cutting back on what they considered frivolous expen-
ditures.

"Relax," Ethan said as she scanned the illuminated com-
mands that would transform her vision into reality. "The
government's just as greedy as private enterprise. Once we
work out the kinks, there's a world of people who'll want to
get their hands on what we've got. We can get funding elsewhere, Eva. Don't sweat it."

"You know I don't want government funding," she
snapped, her nerves on edge and Ethan hitting the most sensitive one. "Not from ours or any of the others that have approached us. They'll want too much control before, during
and after we succeed. Our discovery could be abused, Ethan.
Once absolute virtual reality becomes a reality, it'll be mind
candy—and those who get addicted could easily be controlled by whoever is doling out the sweets."

"Careful. You're sounding like one of our detractors."

They had plenty of those and Eva was all too aware that
some of their fears were warranted. Altered reality wasn't
anything new—like being glued to the tube or getting lost in
a good book or a video game—but those were harmless escapes.

There came a point where escapism wasn't so harmless.

Hooked on fantasy. Forget work, forget family, just check
into Big Brother's holodeck and check out of your worries,
your life. Go where no man has gone before, name your head
trip and we'll name the price.

"They do have some legitimate concerns," she said. "And
that's why it's up to us to make sure that what can be a pos-
itive contribution to humanity isn't turned into a very dangerous tool."

"Has it occurred to you," he said in a hushed whisper, "that we're not immune to some danger ourselves? Especially you? You're the real pioneer and what's in your head is light-years beyond what anyone else exploring cyberspace has come up with. You'd be safer with some protection, Eva."

"I'll take my chances. Besides, I'm no good to anyone if I'm hurt or worse. No need to worry—I'm not." Yet, a part of her was a little uneasy. She'd had the strangest sense of being followed lately. No, not exactly followed, but . . . observed?

It was like an itch she couldn't quite scratch. Just her imagination, she told herself again; the fantasy part of her work overlapping into her sorry excuse for a personal life.

That sorry excuse for a personal life had driven her to indulge herself with what she hoped to offer others who had lost a loved one or needed an imaginary companion because they had none. Lonely days, lonely nights—who needed them?

Eva blew a kiss to the program for luck. Her fantasy man was in it, and he was designed to respond to her in a distinctly male way.

Lord, how she needed that. Badly enough to seek it from a walking-talking puppet she'd ordered up from the hologram bank. Tall, dark and handsome, a great smile. She couldn't touch him without destroying the illusion, but at least he wouldn't be capable of deceit or betrayal, which was more than she could say for her ex-husband, John the Bastard.

Satisfied that everything was as double-checked as it could get, Eva took a deep breath and said, "I'm ready. Keep your fingers crossed, Ethan. This is it."

"I'll keep everything crossed but my legs." He chuckled at her long-suffering glance. "Sorry, just trying to lighten you up. I know we've had a string of failures, but try to remember if this test doesn't click, sooner or later one will." He patted Eva's shoulder at the chamber's entry and she instinctively tensed.

She punched a sequence of numbers on a panel beside the chamber door. It slid open and she stepped inside. *Whoosh.* Sealed within the world of her making, she was separated from everyone and everything in the outside world. The only evidence of its existence was the narrow observatory window, and the camera overhead, almost hidden by a spreading palm tree.

She touched the vivid image of the spiky-barked trunk. Her hand passed through—as it would anything she attempted to touch in the chamber. An optical illusion, all of it. Until she could master the conversion of matter, the holographic settings and animated personae who peopled the holodeck would be little more than smoke and mirrors commanded by a magician with a computerized wand.

Magician that she was, she had done a neat hat trick within this three-dimensional—environment. There was no headgear or gloves suffused with electronic wires to dilute the fantasy.

A balmy breeze blew in from concealed air jets. The sound of birds and trickling water softly cascaded in the background. She willed herself to forget it was an environmental soundtrack rather than the actual sounds of a rain forest. In the thousand-square-foot chamber she was nestled on a rolling carpet of thick grass, and surrounded by hibiscus, green leaves and large exotic flowers.

It was as tranquil and untamed as she longed to be. Surrounded by her fantasy, its lush tropicality induced her to take off her shoes and pretend she could actually feel the springy texture of grass beneath her feet.

Her eyes insisted it was real and she slipped further into the dreamscape, hid herself behind the illuminated cover of foliage. On a whim, she took off her hose, tossed them away in clear view of the camera.

Eva was a little stunned at her own show of naughty behavior—which was also something of a fantasy for her. Trick of lighting though it was, the environment was serving its purpose. Her hold on reality loosening, she could make the mental leap needed to believe in her fantasy man's existence.

If he showed up on cue. *Oh, please, please, don't overload and shut down on me this time. I'll be happy with a word and a wave—I don't even care if nobody sees you but me. Just be!*

Pulse racing madly, she called out, "Companion!"

An eternity of seconds passed and she frantically told herself she'd spoken too softly, that her voice signal to the hologram bank hadn't been picked up. Or maybe the projection distance was more limited than her calculations had indicated.

Then again, maybe the damn thing wasn't working.

Eva ducked beneath a low-hanging tree limb, dewdrops glistening on its still leaves. She was about to repeat her command in a bellowing voice when she felt another force sweep around her.

A subtle shift in the air raised the fine hair on the nape of her neck. Gooseflesh prickled her arms as a wisp of some formidable presence invaded her senses. Impossible. No one was here except her and her imagination.

Closing her eyes and breathing deeply, she inhaled what had to be an imaginary but nonetheless intoxicating scent—clean but earthy, it was purely animal and overwhelmingly male.

"Eva."

Her eyes opened and for the life of her, all she could do was stare. Tall as an Amazon, dark as coffee laced with cream. As for handsome, the computer certainly had some kind of take on its definition.

Somehow she managed to say, "Hi." Well, that should certainly impress him, she thought with an inner wince. But then she reminded herself that he was a 3-D illusion and she was the one in control around here. Or should be. Odd, but she felt as if her brain was sliding, slipping from awareness to the fringes of vague. It was weird. Disorienting.

Suddenly, she swayed. Just as quickly, she was steady on her feet again. No hands were on her but she had the strangest sensation of being held, her arms lightly stroked.

Very strange. And strangely wonderful.

"Hi," she said again and mentally slapped her forehead.

His lips, full and unsparingly sensual, formed a mesmerizing smile. "Hello, Eva. Have you a wish, some pleasure? That is the reason I'm here."

His voice. Never had she heard anything like it, an undulating sound like fine gravel sifted through raw silk. Her own voice sounded unnaturally high and tremulous.

"Sorry if I seem a little-off balance, but . . . well, you're not exactly what I was expecting," she confessed, taking in the overwhelming whole of him.

His eyes were almond-shaped. His brilliant green irises shone like glass as if reflecting some inner light. The ebony mane of his hair was brushed severely back, accentuating the exotic contours of his face. All angles and shadows, he radiated the mystery of the Orient, the ancient secrets of Egypt, the savagery of a stalking wild beast.

As for his clothes... She really should have selected those. All black was fine but they fit indecently well—from the black T-shirt straining on his Tarzan-like chest to his skintight black jeans which left nothing to the imagination.

He stood still, while she gawked. He seemed to take her in just as completely, but did so in a head-to-toe scan, his gaze moving with the speed of a computer rather than the leisurely perusal of a human.

"Do you approve?" he was man enough to ask. Then he grinned, revealing wolverine-sharp incisors—and no lack of confidence in her answer.

"You're, uh . . . fine." She took a little pleasure in the waver of his smile. Her own feminine ego was disgustingly shaky and she needed understanding, not cockiness, to get past what had crippled her confidence. What she needed was a compliment but pride kept her from telling him so. Still, she was needy enough to fish. "What about me? Okay by you?"

"More than 'okay.' You're beautiful."

She'd programmed him to think so. That bothered her now—him feeding her what she needed to hear. A small compliment, if it was honest, meant more than false flattery.

But it wasn't his fault. It was her own.

"Is there some name you want to be called by?" she asked with a heavy sigh.

"You can call me . . . Urich."

"Urich. I like it. And I liked what you said." So, she lied. Eva dug a toe into the grass as evanescent as this whole experience. "You're very generous. Thanks, Urich."

"Why thank me? You don't believe me."

Eva's eyes widened in surprise. He'd actually picked up on her real feelings; whereas computers were notoriously literal.

"How did you know that?"

He paused. A brief sort of click-click consideration.

"Your words were tonally flat. And your expression conveyed disappointment. Some sadness."

Could it be, she wondered, that he might be able to interact with her on a near-human level, after all? If he could interpret shades of emotion through body language and tone, then maybe, just maybe they could get something going.

"You're hopeful now, I see it in your eyes. Look into mine and see that I spoke the truth."

His eyes, those reflective prisms of green, probed hers, held her in thrall. His gaze was so intense, she tried to look away. But couldn't. And then she didn't have the will or the desire. He *did* think she was beautiful, with a conviction so firm she almost believed it herself.

"Belief, Eva, is the key," he murmured. His voice wove through her senses, creating a hypnotic effect. "Tell me that you're beautiful and believe it."

"I...yes. Yes, I *am* beautiful." Did she really say that? The thought slipped away and she knew only that she felt beautiful. He was nodding in approval and Eva vaguely realized she was nodding along with him.

She shook her head, trying to break whatever spell she seemed to be under. Her mind cleared slightly, but she still didn't seem to be quite all there.

Maybe if she passed her hand through him she'd get a better grip on this altered reality that was starting to mess with her head, not to mention her reeling senses. They were insisting he smelled like heaven, and what heaven it would be to bury her face against his neck for a closer inspection.

It was his neck she reached for. But her hands stopped short of contact. Although it seemed they were gently pushed away, something suggested she'd withdrawn them so as not to shatter the illusion of Urich's existence.

How incredibly real he looked. Just as real as herself. Only, she didn't feel very real.

"What are you?" she heard herself say, kind of.

"I'm an extension of your subconscious desires and dreams." His gaze was like a physical touch, an electric sensation making her quiver from the roots of her hair to the soles of her feet. "Talk to me. Tell me about these desires of yours."

"I . . . I want to feel the way I did before my life fell apart and . . . and more. I want so much more."

"To be all that you can be."

"Yes . . . yes."

"It's within your grasp but just escapes your reach. You need me to help you and you'll trust me to do that."

"I need you. I trust you." Her head, it was helium-light, giving her a sense of floating. Something wasn't right. So why did she feel so deliriously fine? She felt . . . peace. A sublime, absolute peace.

You have no fear of me or of yourself.

He hadn't spoken aloud and yet his voice, his tantalizing voice, echoed in her mind.

"I have no fear," she said in a trancelike whisper.

Her reply to his silent command assured Urich that he had breached her subconscious—and with surprising ease. But what surprised him the most was this sudden hesitation to wield his mental powers over her.

He hadn't expected her to be so unresistant, her mind opening like petals to a probing ray of sun. And what he plucked from the recesses of her mind, he hadn't expected at all: vulnerability, self-doubt, fear; a depth and complexity of emotion; sweetness, the simple goodness of her heart. And most certainly *not*, the effect all these things were having on him.

In this moment, he knew Eva better than she knew herself. He also knew that he'd made a gross misjudgment in thinking a calculated study of her habits, ambitions, even her dreams, could have prepared him for the stunning insights into the essence of Eva Campbell. It was his duty, had been his intention, to use such knowledge against her.

And yet, he couldn't bring himself to do it. As for why, it was truly a mystery to him.

A very disturbing mystery. Of all the minds he had probed, as if they were his own, he had never wanted to linger in any after he had obtained what he wanted. But here he was, intrigued and amazed by his greediness for more of this woman.

Even as he heard himself say, "Take down your hair," he wondered at his own impulsive command. And what was this urging he felt, this alien need that had nothing to do with cold ambition, which induced him to murmur: "Your defenses, all of them, let them fall away with the pins."

Urich watched her tug at the pins, then move her head from side to side, shaking out her hair with fluid abandon. And all the while, he kept her transfixed with his unblinking, entrancing gaze. He had to wonder if Eva had worked some deep hypnosis on him. Her eyes, a mixture of sea green and flecks of blue, spoke. And her hair—he was sorely tempted to touch it.

Refusing temptation, he whispered, "It's pretty, so pretty this way. Why do you restrain what should be free?"

"I . . . I need to control everything I can. Even my hair."

"Tell me why."

"Because . . . because deep down I'm afraid if I let go, something bad will happen."

He was glad her defenses were gone, all gone, and that she was confessing to him things she would never confess to another. "You're letting go now, Eva. Letting go . . . letting go. It's a wonderful liberation, one that you need." And she did. Why he took such pleasure in giving her this, Urich didn't know. Perhaps it came from the vicarious thrill of feeling what she felt on this intimate journey. How easily he could take advantage of her now, but her sigh of release touched a chord inside him, an instinct to protect rather than manipulate. "This is a good thing, letting go," he told her, aware that he greatly wished his assurance was true. "Nothing bad will happen, Eva."

"A good thing. Nothing bad will happen."

"That's right," he said, hiding his grimace behind a benevolent smile. "And it's so good that you'll need what you're feeling now, often. I'm the one, Eva, the one who can fill all your needs." He swayed slightly and she followed his sinuous movements. *You need me. Say you'll summon me again.*

She responded to his compelling command. "I will summon you again."

"Soon, Eva. Soon . . . soon . . ."

"Soon," she repeated, taking up his chant.

"Where the hell are you, Eva?" Ethan's urgent yell coincided with a bright flash of light followed by a darkness more absolute than a total eclipse.

Eva shook her head, shook, shook, shook it while Ethan continued to yell. *What had happened?* She was with Urich and they had been talking . . . and . . . and then—

"Oh, no. Oh, no," she cried softly to herself, certain the power had gone off and erased Urich as though he had never been. Unable to accept such a terrible loss, she clung to an imaginary comfort.

Imaginary, to be sure, but every nerve end she possessed insisted she felt a brush against her arm, as consoling as a warm palm, as fleeting as a dream lover's departing blow of a kiss.

2

"WHAT DO YOU MEAN, 'Nothing happened'? Hell, Eva, your hair looks like it went through a wind tunnel and I could hear you muttering to yourself like a crazy lady in there. I gave you a few hours to yourself, just like you wanted, but now I want some answers. *Something* happened, and as second-in-command on this project, I deserve to know what it is."

Lingering over a sip of industrial-strength coffee in her office, Eva debated. She couldn't explain what she didn't understand, and there was much she didn't understand about her encounter with Urich. Disturbingly so. Such as why she still felt energized and yet dazed, transcendentally calm but confused.

Even after splashing enough cold water on her face to wake up from a coma, she felt like she was head-tripping in la-la land. It seemed to have affected her eyesight. She'd stared at the mirror, unable to believe it was her reflection. Her features hadn't changed but there was a radiance about her that was transforming . . . beautiful.

She'd never thought of herself as beautiful before, but beautiful she now believed she was. It was then she remembered Urich telling her that belief was the key. Anything more than that, she drew a blank. All she had was a sense of something profound having occurred, of some rare affinity having been forged with Urich that made her want to refuse all others access to this—this . . . whatever it was they had shared.

As a scientist she was duty-bound to hypothesize and dissect; repeat the experiment and form conclusive answers. But as a woman? She was simply compelled to see him again. Research had nothing to do with it.

Yes, she would see him again . . . soon. And in secret.

But first, she had to appease Ethan.

"Okay," she said slowly, "something did happen. I got caught up in the dreamscape and lost my hold on reality. It was like breathing nitrous oxide in a dentist's chair—being consciously aware of my surroundings while my brain did a free-fall."

"Lucid dreaming in a waking state?"

"Exactly. VR can be disorienting, but I'm acclimatized to it. This went beyond anything I've ever experienced before."

"Interesting. Any idea how it happened?"

Eva had more than an idea; she was certain Urich had been instrumental in the process. But she pretended to think it over, then shook her head.

"Unfortunately, no. But it definitely bears examination. There could be some psychological repercussions from holodeck usage we need to check out."

"That's not our concern, Eva."

"The hell it's not!" She thunked down her mug and coffee splattered onto the newest government inquiry littering her desk. "Our responsibilities don't end with just turning out a successful invention that could—"

"Change reality as mankind knows it," Ethan supplied by rote. "God, you are such a bleeding heart. When are you going to realize that we are not psychologists, sociologists or ethics instructors? We're physics and computer experts, scientists whose only responsibility is discovery, not the policing of humanity's use or misuse of it."

Here we go again, she thought wearily. This was where they always collided before Ethan subtly pushed for government funding. His only concern was obtaining more financial means in order to reach their collaborative end.

But it wasn't as collaborative as he thought. Urich wasn't the only thing Eva was keeping to herself.

"I refuse to get into this today," she said with a pointed glance at her watch. "Look, it's getting late and the sooner you leave, the sooner I can figure out where I screwed up with the animated hologram's program."

"Sorry it didn't work," he said sympathetically while his gaze darted to a page of calculations she discreetly covered.

"Me, too. Later, Ethan."

At the door, he paused. "Why don't you call it a day like everyone else did an hour ago? C'mon, Eva, let's lock this place up and go get a beer. I'll buy."

"Thanks, but I'll take a rain check."

"Hey, don't be mad at me."

"I'm not mad." No, she simply wanted him to scram so she could make tracks to the computer.

"I wish you'd come with me," he urged. "I always worry a little when you stay late by yourself."

"That's sweet, Ethan. But you've done a bang-up job with the security system and no uninvited guests can get past it without an entrée from me or you. Really, I'll be fine."

When Ethan still hesitated, she pointed an imperious finger at the door and ordered, "Leave!"

He pouted like a rejected suitor but finally, *finally* left. After a prudent wait, she searched the building for any signs of stragglers. Ten researchers and one secretary, gone.

Deeming it safe, she hurried to the master computer. But once there, Eva hesitated.

She'd been so disoriented when the power went off that it had taken a while to realize Urich could be called up again. What she didn't know was if their encounter had been saved.

Now was the time to find out if some of those details she continued to comb her brain for were in his memory.

Just as she was about to boot up the program, she sensed she wasn't alone. She glanced over her shoulder.

No one. So why this eerie sensation? Eva shivered. The temperature seemed to have suddenly dropped, the way it supposedly did at the appearance of a ghost.

She'd never seen one and the scientist in her gave little credence to psychic phenomena. And yet ... Urich had seemed to have some strange influence over her that reason continued to insist wasn't possible. But matter conversion was supposedly impossible, too. And she was close, so damn close to opening that Pandora's box ... it was chilling. Yet damn exhilarating.

Eva swiped her palms over her skirt. She was sweating. The room was cold and she was burning up—as if her internal thermostat had leaped ten degrees higher in a matter of seconds.

Forget checking out the memory of her encounter with Urich. She needed some fresh air.

Outside, she deeply inhaled the early-fall breeze. A drive to the waterfront sounded good. The bay always soothed her with its healing magic; there she could get body and soul together again.

Her thoughts were on Urich and the day's mysteries as she drove. But when she pulled up in front of to her modest Victorian two-story house in her equally modest sedan, Eva wondered where her mind had been. She hadn't meant to drive home, but home she was.

Another mystery to add to the rest? Nonsense. There was surely a rational explanation for everything, including this.

She did have a bad habit of driving on automatic pilot. And this wasn't the first time she wasn't conscious of how she got to where she was going. It happened to a lot of people, right? Right. But still, zoning out behind the wheel was dangerous, and thank heaven she hadn't had an accident.

So, where to from here? Inside there would be that awful dread silence. No classical music playing in the background or pots and pans banged in the kitchen. No cheating husband coming from that direction with a kiss and a lie on his lips. She didn't want to face another empty night in her empty house with only the glow of a computer screen for company. It wasn't enough and she was sick of pretending it was.

Encountering Urich had brought an unexpected intrigue to her day, her life.

"Well, are you going to the waterfront or are you getting your buns inside to change for the fantasy date of your life?" There she went again, talking to herself. "He talks back, the water just listens. But the water's a lot safer than getting in deeper with something you can't explain. Yet."

It came to her that the only real way to find out what she was dealing with was to go to the source itself.

The car continued to idle while Eva gave that some thought. She couldn't discount the danger she was courting. Lucid dreaming, indeed. She was still buzzing from the rush.

Getting hooked on some mind candy herself was a frightful possibility. But to subject others to any hazards her creation might unleash without taking the risk first would make her no better than a mad scientist setting Frankenstein on the loose.

Screw Ethan. *She* was calling the shots. Another program would take Urich's place for the documented experiments. But tonight the chamber would be hers and Urich's.

Eva cut the engine. "Soon," she whispered. "Soon..."

"SHE WANTS TO SEE YOU again," Raven said approvingly.

Urich held his silence, knowing if he said anything it would betray his newfound distaste for their eavesdropping. Neither did he like their watching her, as they did now, monitoring Eva's return to her place of work, appearance significantly altered.

Such dislike for these necessary measures, which he'd considered interesting, even amusing before, was a signal that he was losing his objectivity. Otherwise he'd be feeling quite pleased with the influence he already had over her—evident in her labors to create another illusionary stage and not bothering to check the program's memory.

As for his memory, it contained much that it shouldn't. Pleasure in her company and the beauty of her, without and within. Oh, yes, he thought Eva was beautiful; an absolutely delightful creature who hadn't a clue of her unique allure. He could alter that, as easily as she changed the setting. Again.

It didn't take a mind reader to surmise the mood she was in. When she selected a stage he thought particularly appealing, he prompted her to keep it.

With a glance at Raven, he noted a look of envy. And an unmistakable eagerness to view the approaching event.

Urich switched off the spying device. It was an impulsive decision that startled him as much as it apparently did Raven, upon being informed, "I'll give you a full report when I return."

"What! Urich, this isn't according to plan!"

"The plan is for me to gain her trust, and once I do..." Why did he feel this aversion to discussing their mission? And why did he no longer relish being the one who would hand her over to the powers-that-be, who would then use her for a most worthy purpose. Yes, worthy. But their nation's future would be at Eva's expense. Willing or not, once he delivered her, she wouldn't be allowed to leave. Golden her cage would be, yet she'd be no less a prisoner.

Ah, deductive reasoning—a logical explanation for his aversion. But that didn't make the aversion go away.

Wishing he could clear his mind of this troubling matter as easily as he did his throat in the tense silence, Urich held his ground. "The plan has changed slightly, Raven. No surveillance tonight. I'll know if you watch, and should your doubt in me compel you to observe, then you'll have to find a more trustworthy replacement."

"You know there is no one who can replace you."

"Which is why you'll agree to humor me." *Was he actually saying this?* He couldn't believe his own words any more than the consuming fascination with Eva that had provoked them.

"But you might have need for our protection," Raven ventured, eyeing him as though he'd grown two heads.

And perhaps he had. Urich suddenly wondered if he had possessed Eva's mind only for her mind to do some possessing of its own. He was, after all, fixing his gaze on Raven's hand, which hovered over the screen. A slight jerk of his head and Raven's hand was thrust back, held paralyzed in midair.

"I can protect myself, Raven," he said with a thin smile. "Shall we allow Dr. Campbell to test the true capabilities of her program? Or would you rather me disengage it and appear on command? Your choice. But I suggest a quick decision since she'll be expecting me . . . soon."

Raven muttered a curse. No one dared usurp his authority. No one, Urich amended, but this ungodly new self that seemed to be taking him over and eradicating his reason.

"A full report will be expected," Raven growled.

"Certainly." Assured of the privacy he had won for himself and Eva, Urich relaxed. Then, departing swiftly, he wondered if he had promised more than he would be inclined to deliver.

HIS SECOND BREACHING of the premises was as easy as the first. Child's play, really, but there was nothing that simple about Eva, or what she stirred in him while he watched her natural gravitation toward him, still unaware of his presence.

He could fool others into thinking him invisible. A parlor trick, but one he disdained to use as she glided through the chamber sprinkled with stars against void.

The stars were like Eva. They shimmered with a luminous brilliance, but couldn't see their own magnificence. He saw hers. She was a vision wrapped in a flowing white diaphanous dress, calling "Companion."

How he wished he could be that to her. How he wished he didn't have this unexpected and unwelcome need for a companion of his own.

Blending into the void's shadow, Urich allowed himself to savor the sight of her while he grappled with the duplicity of the role his ambition had led him to fill. So much for ambition. It was fast becoming regret.

"Companion," she called again, the urgency in her voice echoing his own need to touch her. Her hair, her mind. And oh, to touch her breasts, her beautiful breasts . . .

"Compan—" Eva stopped in mid-command. *He was here.* She sensed it in the air's shift, waves of energy rippling over its current. Over her. She looked from one bare arm to the other, gooseflesh rising with the sensation of fingertips sweeping up their tender undersides, then grazing her neck.

She should be uneasy, feeling a Twilight Zone sort of apprehension. Yet she was arching her neck, thrilling to a phantom touch. It was exquisite. Unearthly. It was such heaven.

"I know you're here." She also knew his memory had been saved; the atmosphere was warm and familiar. *Lord, when did you become a psychic?* Hardly that, but she nonetheless *knew.* "You *are* here," Eva said with more force.

"How did you know?" From deep in the shadows came that marvelous voice she could listen to for eternity and beyond.

"I felt you."

"Considering you can't see or touch me, isn't that a rather unscientific observation to make?"

She started to point out that atomic structure was invisible but was accepted as fact. Eva shelved it. Any discussions on quantum theory she'd save for Ethan. Urich had the ability to discuss it, too, but that wasn't the purpose of their visit tonight. She needed answers. Almost as much as she needed his company and this inexplicable feeling of hands sifting through her hair.

"I felt you," she insisted. "I still do."

"Interesting. Assuming that I could actually defy your beloved laws of physics . . . did you, do you, like it?"

She *adored* it. But Urich seemed to be toying with her. Subtly poking fun at the profession he had to thank for his existence.

"Fine. It's . . . fine," she said.

You like it, Eva. You like it a lot. And so do I.

Had she thought that? Of course, she'd thought it, but she could swear it was Urich's voice she'd heard.

"Did you say something? But not say it?" The question sounded crazy even to her. No wonder he was quietly laughing.

"That makes two. So far."

"Two what?"

"Less-than-scientific observations. But they could bear investigating. Maybe we should—make it a game of sorts."

"The last thing I want to talk about are scientific observations. And enough of this head game!" Striding into the darkness, the stars behind her, she demanded, "Where are you?"

"Here. Making an observation of my own."

His voice was as close as a tap on her shoulder. *What did he do, leapfrog over her?* Momentarily stunned, Eva was rooted in place. The best she could do was whisper, "And what kind of observation would your own be?"

"That you are stunning." The air against her back was pure energy, bouncing from him to her like a kinetic heartbeat. "Eva, not even the stars can compete."

3

SLOWLY, EVER SO slowly she turned, scintillating sensation
washing over her as she did.

Awed by the sheer majesty of him, Eva felt graced simply
to behold his presence.

No wonder she felt so light-headed; all the questions she'd
prepared were vacating her brain as she stood here, drinking
him in and basking in his outrageous compliment

But there it was again. In his eyes. He believed what he had
said. And strangely, she felt worthy of his praise.

"Thank you, Urich." _How did he do it?_ How did he make
her feel so radiant, transformed? "You have a peculiar effect
on me—a good one—but I can't help but wonder . . . how?"

"It might be easier to explain if you described this 'peculiar effect' I'm causing."

"To begin with, I feel like I'm hooked up to a socket, only
it's more of a sensory sizzle than a shock."

"Hmm. You must be reacting to my energy source—similar to static crackling fabric or lifting hair." He passed a hand
high over her crown and her hair stood on end. It danced
back and forth, following the wave of his palm.

Her roots tingled in playful, pleasurable delight. Eva
laughed as she imagined the sight she made.

Urich grinned. "I can distance myself if you don't like me
to sizzle your senses."

"No!" she protested when he began to move away—more
a fluid shifting of form, like he was moonwalking, than stepping back. Holograms weren't bound by the same laws of

nature and gravity as humans, she knew. Eva also knew she didn't want him to be a hologram, didn't even want to think it. Too late, she had.

Her laughter faded and she regarded Urich with longing. She longed for him to be real, longed to be able to touch him.

All the more reason to crack that Pandora's box. Until then, she'd just have to pretend and content herself with the marvels of the mysterious. Things that could surely be explained, just as Urich had with his cause-and-effect demonstration. But then the mystique would be gone.

Eva decided she'd rather enjoy the magical. Fairy dust. As a child she'd hoped against hope that Tinker Bell would sprinkle some on her so she could fly. But like Wendy she'd grown up, while Peter Pan soared on, forever young, believing in fairy dust.

With an impish smile, Eva pretended it was fairy dust she scattered as she swept her right arm around in an arc. "Never-Never Land. How do you like it?"

"I like it almost as much as I like you. I feel quite at home."

"Like they say, home is where the heart is."

"And where is yours, Eva?"

There went the fairy dust. "Actually, Urich, my heart's belonged to this place so long that I'm not sure how to act, even in the company of a . . ." She couldn't bring herself to say it. "With you."

"Call me a 'man' if you want. We both know I'm something other than that, but then again, you're more than a woman."

"John said I was less than a woman," she muttered, immediately wishing back the words.

"John was a fool."

Anger chipped his tone. It was gratifying to hear but was also a curious reaction. "Since you don't know him, why do you seem so incensed with the man?"

"He obviously hurt you. And even convinced you of what is totally untrue."

Was it really? Eva wondered. In the three years since she had found John in bed with another woman, she had tried desperately to convince herself his accusations weren't true. But her self-esteem was so wounded that she had shut out all men, for fear another would also find her lacking.

Urich wasn't capable of making that judgment call. Suddenly she wished that he could, that his perception of her wasn't skewed by the influence she had exercised.

There was no way around it. She might as well enjoy the much-needed boost to her ego and a waiting ear to unload on. And he did seem to be waiting, wanting her to say something.

"You're right, Urich. He not only ripped my heart out, John convinced me that I lack worth. Not professionally—I know I'm the best at what I do here. But as a woman? I feel like dry goods on the shelf of a life put on hold. More than anything, I want to sink my teeth into it and taste all that I can." If only she could taste Urich. Mmm, mmm. "Maybe even some forbidden fruit," she added with a wistful sigh.

"The only one keeping you from that, is you."

"Don't I know it. Sometimes I wonder if I'd been more open, more adventurous, just—just *more*, then maybe I would have been enough for John."

"You're taking responsibility for his weakness. Why?"

A good question from a very insightful . . . man. "The hell if I know. I let him treat me like dirt and I hate him for that, really hate him. Sometimes I almost hate myself for ever letting anyone have that kind of power over me."

"Power," Urich murmured, "takes many forms. Your own power is much greater than you realize. It's inside you, but you lock it away. Just as you do your needs."

"How do you know all this?"

"Eyes are windows. In yours I see all this and more."

She should feel uncomfortable, being read like a wide-open book. But instead, it was truly liberating to be so understood, so accepted as she was. Still, as with most people, there was much about herself she avoided contemplating.

A master gleaner Urich seemed to be, so she was both eager and apprehensive as she asked, "What more do you see?"

His eyes probed hers with an intensity almost too piercing to endure. She had the strangest sense of falling.

"A formidable creature, that's what I see," he said quietly, his voice having the effect of a pendulum's lulling swing. "She's regal and she's bold. A being of untamed desires and awesome courage. This is who you really are, Eva. Who you can be—once you find a way to set her free."

Was she hallucinating? Eva wondered. She could see the creature he described—a lioness within, a woman who reveled in the power she asserted to claim her every dream. Expression triumphant and fierce, arms lifted to the night sky as if it were hers to rule, who was this stunning creature?

And then Eva realized, it was . . . her. She must be in that same trancelike state, but how marvelous was the free-fall of her mind, leaping past stifling defenses and seducing her to embrace this ether world of lush sensation and sweet, languorous peace.

She wanted to stay here, with Urich, forever . . . evermore. . . . "Where are we?" she asked from what seemed a great distance, her words sounding like pebbles rippling on a pond.

"In a place that exists within the realm of your mind." His voice flowed through her veins like an opiate laced with adrenaline. "It's in your mind that you create your own reality. As simple as mind over matter. Mind over matter."

"Mind . . . over . . . matter," she repeated.

"Yes, Eva. Wherever you want to go, whatever you want to do or whoever you long to be, it's all within your reach. Reach now and find what it is you really want. What does Eva Campbell *want?* Tell me."

"I want . . ." There was so much that she wanted. She wanted to be that lioness. She wanted to be lonely no more. Urich—she wanted to touch him as intimately, as completely as he had her. "I want to know you as you know me."

She thought he hesitated, but couldn't be sure. Time had no meaning, the way it was in dreams. Was she dreaming? If so, the chamber was where the dream was unfolding. And somehow Urich was accessing the hologram bank to create a dazzling laser-light picture.

"First, I want you to see us as I do," he said, sounding very real as he drew an image of parallel lines that danced in separate, sinuous waves. He clasped his hands and the lines intersected. Looping together, neon blue pulsed against a sea of black and incandescent stars.

"We're lonely creatures, Eva. Prisoners, both of us—to our fates, our abilities and visions. Our worlds couldn't be more different, but how alike we are."

"Are we?" she asked, wondering if they were really having this conversation. Dream or no dream, she felt no need to guard her words or question his, and what a delicious treat that was. "Get up, get dressed, go to work. Work, work, work. Go to bed, get up, get dressed, then back to work again. Are we really alike that way?"

He chuckled once, but it wasn't a happy sound, as if he were laughing at himself and without humor.

"I'm here, aren't I? Trapped as surely as you. But Eva, even prisoners like us can escape to a place no one else can go, unless we allow them in. If you really want to know me as I know you, then . . . welcome. Look deep, deep into my eyes and see who I am, what I can be."

She felt like Alice stepping through his looking-glass gaze, only there was no white rabbit to chase, just this sense of sliding from one dimension and into another. Into Urich, into his skin, into his holograph world. It was a vista composed of kaleidoscope color, laser-light brilliant.

"So much color," she whispered. "What does it mean?"

"It's the landscape of my soul," he said in what had to be a dream, one she never wanted to awaken from. "I wasn't sure if I had one, but it seems you've created more than I'm supposed to be. Go ahead, Eva, tell me what you see."

"Red. Bright and—and angry. Rage?"

"Oh, yes, our situation makes me very angry." His low growl of frustration emerged before Urich could control it. Then absolute silence, absolute stillness, while he allowed Eva to see him as he would never permit another. Madness, sheer madness. His only claim to logic was exposing his true colors in hologram form—as if her scientific labor of love could actually produce what Eva so astutely perceived:

A silver valor. Black as death and white so pure it was blinding. Blue was a livid bruise, a heartache to rival her own. And passion—his was the color of a full moon eclipsed by a consuming sun. This she told him with a throaty sigh, a tremulous moan to his own silent groan.

Urich quickly shut his eyes, effectively sealing her out while he groped for some shred of reason to block this disaster in the making.

"Take me back," she demanded. "Let me see more."

He didn't dare. Yet impulse and instinct impelled him to fill himself with the sight of her, find some way to touch her without giving himself away. With one look, one fateful look,

Eva's eyes searching his and echoing his own yearning need, Urich knew he *had* to touch her.

"There's more," he slowly confirmed. "Much more. But is it real? Or only a fantasy?" He knew he was playing with her head, and she was only semiconscious—thanks to his suppression of her beta brain waves—but this way they could have their stolen piece of cake and eat it, too. "And does it really matter? After all, *you* are my fantasy. A forbidden fantasy, Eva."

"Forbidden? I don't understand."

"It's really simple." Hardly that, but he had to make her think so. Or put her completely under and leave. Return to Raven, surely waiting for his report? Or stay? Foolish as it was, he'd give in to temptation this once. Just once. "I'm not supposed to be able to touch you, or you, me. But fantasies aren't bound by reality, are they?"

"No," she agreed, vaguely. He urged her further into the Theta realm, but not too far since he certainly didn't want her asleep. As desperate as he was to simply touch her, something was holding him back. Maybe he had a conscience after all, making him feel a definite wrongness in laying hands on Eva without her being aware of his actions.

Testing her coherence, he asked, "Do you remember what I said, about mind over matter?"

Eva nodded, in a fluid, deeply relaxed movement. "We create our own realities...in our minds. Only, what is reality? I...I don't know anymore. Do you?"

Definitely coherent, but extremely susceptible to suggestion. Perfect. He had her where he wanted her, but he had to tread with care. It was consent, not coercion, that would make whatever they might share right.

"As the world knows it, reality is an illusion."

"Then what is illusion?"

"For us, for now . . ." His head lowered and he willed her to meet his gaze once more. A hunger so deep it was ravenous awaited her there, but the palm he cupped to her cheek was as tender as the ache of his longing for this touch.

"Illusion, Eva," he whispered, "is *reality*."

"EVA?"

"Mmm . . . Urich," she murmured, sliding her hands over his . . . chest? No, she was touching something harder, and her head was on it, too.

Her own shoulders were being shaken. Urgently. And someone was saying, "Eva! Eva, wake up!"

Ethan's voice. Ethan? Ethan!

Blinking furiously in the harsh fluorescent lighting, Eva realized she was in her office, slumped in her chair.

Bolting upright, she demanded, "What time is it?"

"Two in the morning," he said, eyeing her strangely. "What are you doing here?"

What *was* she doing here? Why wasn't she in Urich's arms, her lips to his neck and his in her hair? But . . . no, it wasn't possible.

It's in your mind that you create your own reality. His words echoed, giving her pause. Had it all been a dream? Had she actually driven herself here, gone into some delusional episode in the chamber, then sleepwalked her way to her desk? *No.* She wasn't psychotic and never in her life had she sleepwalked. So how did she explain what *had* occurred?

Clearly, Urich had some sort of inside track into the workings of the mind—at least the one that had given birth to him. Preposterous. But *what if,* what if there really was a place within the psyche that contained the powers she *distinctly* remembered Urich saying she possessed? Then, yes, then

Urich could possibly become real, in every sense, within her mind.

Eva rolled her eyes. Far be it from her to discount any discovery unknown to man, but actually reaching a place where anything imaginable could be experienced as totally real?

Taking a steadying breath, she tried to concentrate on Ethan. He looked uneasy as she assessed him with the same sort of probing vision that was unique to Urich. *Urich, Urich. It always comes back to Urich.*

"I was working and fell asleep," she said, aware of a calmness that slightly unnerved her. "That explains me, but aren't you a little early to be clocking in?"

"I, uh...I was on my way home from the bar when I passed by and saw your car. Thought I'd check up on you."

"As you can see, I'm fine."

He stared at her oddly, took a step back, and kept staring. *What was the matter with him?* He was looking at her as if she had taken on the form of a predator ready to pounce and was half hoping she would.

"Are you sure? You . . . you don't seem quite yourself."

Well, thank God for that, she wanted to say. She was, in fact, feeling quite beyond her usual self. Confident and bold, a woman fully realized, sustained by her sense of inner peace and wisdom. Her *power.*

"Oh, really? How do I seem different?"

"I don't know exactly, but you do." He laughed nervously. "Maybe it's the clothes. Guess you went out after all and came back here?"

"Something like that. Anything else different about me?" she pressed, wondering if she looked as different as she felt.

"The hair, definitely the hair. And...and your face. That's it, your face. You look like you're glowing."

"Must be the lighting," she offered, although she did feel as if she had swallowed a star and was glowing with the light of the cosmos.

She stood and Ethan edged toward the door. "Since you're okay, guess I'll be going." He rubbed his hands together, an awkward gesture that matched his hesitation. "But I can stick around while you pack up, walk you to your car."

"Thanks, but I have some more work I want to get done." As she indicated the piles of paper on her desk, her gaze fell on a sheet with three large words, scrawled in her handwriting. Forcing a polite, "Good night, Ethan," she waited for the sound of his footsteps, then seized the page. In her grip it shook, as did her whispered: *"Mind over matter."*

"FINALLY YOU'RE BACK, Urich." Anxiety sharpened Raven's voice as he padded across the floor of his private quarters.

Resigned to an interrogation, Urich gave a small bow.

"I'm sorry for waking you."

"No apology needed." With hope, Raven added, "I'm sure your delay is justified."

"It is," Urich confirmed. What he didn't say was that his delay had been due to some painful self-examination. He had crossed a line with Eva that left him straddled between loyalty to his people, wanting her for himself, and truly caring about her needs, not the least of which was her right to freedom. And what had all his soul-searching netted him? Nothing but a stalemate of emotional confusion—guilt for his betrayal to the mission; absolute rapture; and absolute regret for having held the woman he never should have touched.

Disguising his inner turmoil with a detached facade, Urich heard the lie leave his lips. "She's elusive. It could take a while for me to convince Eva that her future belongs with us."

Raven raised a speculative eyebrow. "Eva, is it? Do I detect a personal interest in Dr. Campbell that doesn't bode well for your delivery of her to us?"

"The success of this mission depends on my ability to win her trust in me." And he was winning it, winning it so quickly and easily, and not deserving her trust at all. "It's her nature to trust those she has a personal affinity with. You know this as well as I do, Raven," he said, further compromising himself. "Therefore, why should you disapprove of the relationship I was ordered to form with . . . Dr. Campbell?"

Raven met his challenging glare. Unable to withstand Urich's visual lancing, he began to stalk the room, his copious silver hair swishing with the weary shake of his head.

Urich noticed the stiffened measure of his gait, the slight slump in Raven's shoulders, still proud but heavy with the burden of more than his age. He looked as though he carried the weight of a dying race in his arms—one he couldn't let go any more than he could continue on.

"You trouble me, Urich. Always, always you've troubled me with the powers you possess and the isolation you covet. But never have you troubled me as you do now. Even I, who can't search your mind, can perceive the . . . affection? Yes, the affection you have for this woman."

"Affection isn't something I'm familiar with," he hedged.

"Then, since you feel none, you wouldn't be averse to abducting her?"

"*No*. I won't do such a thing, Raven." He took a menacing step forward. "And neither will you."

"Ah, Urich, there it is. The source of my concern. You're becoming protective and possessive of her. Such attachment will cloud your judgment. And it's bound to cause problems once she joins our fold. We need her for a greater purpose than your own desires dictate."

It was true, all of it. He wanted to demand they stop this atrocious plan, but no, here he was composing his face into an implacable mask and denying every rightful charge.

"My desires dictate that she come willingly to us. Should she be abducted, she'll be resistant and our greater purpose will suffer for it."

Raven was silent for a telling length of time. When he finally spoke, it was with the skill of a swordsman cleanly spearing the most vulnerable point of a comrade well-known.

"As always, your judgment is sound. No wonder I regard you with a respect few others command. Proceed with Dr. Campbell—or rather, Eva—as you deem most advantageous to our mutual goal. We *are* relying on you and I'm certain it's an entrustment well placed." He paused meaningfully. "If you like, we'll do away with any surveillance of your meetings—your loyalty being without question. Accept my gratitude for your service to our people, and the success I know you'll achieve."

Urich bowed and quickly cut a path to the door. But before he could escape, Raven struck another velvet blow.

"By the way, your father wants to see you. Zar will be so pleased when you relay the progress you made tonight."

The door trembled slightly, the force of Urich's distress beating at its surface like a pounding fist as Raven added, "In exchange for your typically sage advice, perhaps you'll accept a bit of mine. Before you see Zar, might I suggest that you see to your appearance? There's an imprint on your neck—several of them, in fact. Red and slightly smeared, but they do bear a curious resemblance to lips."

STARING OUT AT THE STARS, so like the illusion that had surrounded him and Eva, Urich smacked the glassy barrier.

Pacing, pacing, searching for answers and none forthcoming. *Why* had he let her into his most secret place, shared his very essence and absorbed her kindred spirit as if it were rain to feed the drought of his soul? It had been empty, so empty for so long that he had become like the void, feeling no joy, no pain. An infinity of nothingness.

Until Eva had filled him with her substance. What a fool he had been to partake of what he couldn't keep. Yes, only a fool would have slipped into her deepest reaches and grasped the woman within, the whole of her so fine and glorious.

And the innocence of her, gathered so trustingly in his arms; the press of her lips to his neck . . .

Urich stroked where she had marked him. He had begrudged each swipe of the cloth ridding him of her traces; yet forever would he remember the power of her intimate touch.

"Power," he snarled, spitting out the word as if he could trample upon its fickle composition. How well he knew the powers of the mind. But they were as nothing, *nothing*, compared to the dangerous influence a heart could wield.

He had thought his heart immune to such human weakness. How wrong he had been. And now he was paying for it—and dearly. His visit with Raven had been pure pleasure compared to what that with his father would be.

Trapped, that's what he was. Trapped in a cage of his own making, having no one but himself to blame from start to finish.

With a snort of self-derision, he wondered what insanity had possessed him to let Eva to retain all they had shared—save his carrying her to the office, almost crushing her with a consuming embrace, then departing with a command to sleep deeply and dream of him.

Urich dropped his face into his hands. What was done was done. But he would not, could not, repeat that mistake. His responsibilities were clear and there was no margin for compromise. When next he saw Eva, his heart must be hardened.

It twisted painfully, revolting against his vow.

"I WILL NOT GO to the chamber," Eva vowed. "I will not go to the chamber. I will not—" She stopped in mid-mantra. That rap at the door could only be Ethan. Jeez, but she wished he'd get a life outside of work.

Good advice, Eva. Listen to it and take up a hobby, join a club, just get the hell out of here and go mingle with some real people. "Shut up," she muttered to that nasty little voice nagging at her again before calling out, "Come in."

The door swung open and there was Ethan, of course. And of course, he was pushing up his glasses, then swinging back his mop of hair and slouching against the doorframe, hands shoved in pockets, Mr. Wannabe Cool posture assumed.

"I'm not leaving without you tonight," he announced. "You owe me a rain check on yesterday's beer and on top of that, we hit a breakthrough today—"

"A minor one." She sounded as bitchy as she felt. Eva blamed Urich for that. If she didn't have him to compare the other hologram with, she'd be smiling big instead of glowering at poor Ethan. "The hologram didn't talk."

"But it did show up on cue. *And* it moved."

"I'll say," she grumbled. "The damn thing was all over the place—Jim Carey on speed with his tongue cut out!"

"Hey, there's more than one way to change reality as mankind knows it." Ethan gave her a boyish grin that revealed the braces he usually tried so hard to hide. He was trying to cheer her up and the least she could do was fake a smile. "Much better. Now listen up. We're celebrating whether you like it or not. Not only did we have—okay, a minor—breakthrough, I get my braces off tomorrow. The first round's on me." He unhooked her jacket and flapped it like a matador enticing a charging bull. "As for the second, we can flip a coin if you're in one of your Gloria Steinem moods."

Well, well, it seemed Ethan could get pushy if he put his mind to it. *Mind*. Mind over matter. Damn, why didn't she just burn the paper that had seared its message into her brain as surely as a hologram named Urich had screwed with her head.

A day. One day and one inexplicable night had passed. It seemed like a lifetime since she'd seen Urich and yet it seemed like he'd never quite left her.

If she didn't leave, not all the mantras in the world would keep her away from the chamber. Hell, Eva decided, if Urich was some kind of spook in disguise—yet another "Yeah, right" hypothesis to log in with the rest—let him follow her to the bar. She was out of here.

AN HOUR LATER, all Eva could think was *I want out of here!* Ethan's choice of bar was one of those grunge-rock places. Tunes she'd never heard blasted from a CD jukebox; as for the neohippie attire sported by much of the crowd, her own black slacks and white turtleneck seemed outdated.

Ditto for her volume tolerance. The music competed with arcade games that apparently doubled as dance-floor space. Getting down from atop a pinball machine was a pencil-thin waif in army boots and saggy jeans with rips in the knees.

She hated this place. It made her feel *old*.

"The sixties don't look any better now than they did back then," Eva muttered sourly before taking a sip of the warm beer she was still nursing.

"Say again?" Ethan leaned across the table with the same eagerness he'd shown every time she uttered a word.

What was with him tonight? The way he kept urging her to drink up and cut loose for a change made her wonder if he was trying to get her drunk so he could pick her brain for those secret calculations he wasn't above snooping for.

How cynical, Eva thought with a twinge of guilt. Ethan was simply being sociable and she was grouchy because she was in withdrawal from her mind-candy fix.

Forcing her mind from the chamber's temptation, she pointed to the jukebox and said, "I was wondering what kind of music is *that?*"

"That's Trent Reznor. You know, Nine Inch Nails."

No, she didn't know. Which just went to show how out of touch she was with the life she needed to get outside of work.

Then again, maybe not! The lyrics assaulting her were appalling. Surely she hadn't heard right.

"Ethan, did I just hear what I thought I heard?" she asked, mouth agape.

"Uh . . . yeah," he said, sporting a sudden blush.

Eva could feel her own cheeks heating up as the singer—if she could call it singing—once again shrieked that he wanted to "do it" like an animal—or rather, "do you"—and the "do" part was about as bathroom-stall graphic as it got.

The lyrics were embarrassing enough, but what really disturbed her was the image of this most basic act of nature, becoming just that. Raw and primal, without the inhibitions that divided animal from man. *What would it be like?* Even as she wondered, Eva was stunned to feel the lick of arousal. It made her uncomfortable, especially since it sprang from a song that was downright disgusting.

"How about a video game?" Ethan asked as the song faded out and she searched for an excuse to fade out herself.

Glancing at the nearby arcade area, Eva noticed the waif on the pinball machine was eyeing Ethan and swiveling her hips in his direction. A chance to escape? Yes!

"I think she has designs on you, Ethan."

"Designs?" He tossed back his hair, scrunched up his brow—apparently stumped by a term that preceded *dude.*

"She wants to get something going," Eva explained. "As in, see me hit the road so she can introduce herself." Grabbing her purse, she promptly plunked down a ten, and got up, jacket still on. "The rest of the night's on me. I'd wish you luck, but I don't think you need it. Something tells me she'll bring her own glass."

With freedom a step away, she paused—then said the only nice thing she'd said all day: "Oh, and congratulations on getting rid of those braces. I know they bother you. But Ethan, with or without them, you'll always be the same to me—a sweetheart who not only puts up with my moods, you're *cute*."

With that, Eva took off. Once outside, she sighed her relief and waved to Ethan at their table near the front. He didn't see, Eva noted with a smile. He had company. Good for them, she thought, the night was young and so were they.

She wished she could say the same for herself. Thirty-four wasn't really very old, but somewhere, somehow, she'd lost the vital spark that was the true measure of youth, no matter one's years. Urich made her feel young. And confused. And scared. And beautiful and brave and alive as never before. And she had to stop thinking about him, get some distance and take back control.

"I will not go to the chamber," she chanted, cranking the engine of her modest sedan that would take her to her modest home—all so predictable, all so very *her*.

As she drove, Eva chastised herself for so meanly judging Ethan's social maturity when her own was hardly better. After all, here she was stopping at the video store and renting *Ace Ventura, Pet Detective*. Then home again, home again, jiggedy-jig—especially around the hips that could stand to lose two inches since she'd rather ignore them than work out with the leotard-lithe crowd. Loads of butter on the popcorn, great for depression, a VCR with remote control—what more could a woman want?

What does Eva Campbell want?

Stuffing her face with megafat grams only made her feel more empty. And the sound from the tube was grating on ears that were desperate to hear Urich's voice.

How long could she stay away from the chamber? Once there, Urich could work her mind like the remote control she clenched. Eva held it tight, like a security blanket, needing to control something.

GET UP, GET DRESSED, go to work. Work, work, working, and not getting a damn thing done—except for doodles of hearts and cursive swirls of Urich's name on a page that read: "Mind over Matter."

"I will not go to the chamber. I will not go to the chamber—" Knock, knock. Sure it was Ethan, she slipped the telltale paper into the book she'd checked out from the library during lunch, locked her desk, and went for the door.

"Hi, Ethan. Bye, Ethan."

"I was just about to leave myself." He shoved his hands in his pockets and hesitated at her office exit. "Want me to walk you to your car?"

Afraid he'd suggest some more after-work schmoozing, Eva made her excuses. "That's okay. I want to check something out on the hologram bank before I take off." And because she wanted to do just that, and *badly*, she was going home pronto.

Thankfully, he didn't put up a fuss, but said agreeably, "You go ahead and I'll make sure everything's locked up."

FOUR DAYS. Four nails-bitten-to-the-quick days and she hadn't given in to temptation.

It was constant, a compulsive urge to be fought.

The urge was winning tonight.

Eva rubbed her eyes, then slammed shut the book that had strained them. Glancing around her bedroom, it seemed emptier than usual, almost as empty as she felt.

That odd, wondrous glow had faded with the same slipping pull of the sun swallowed by the horizon. She wanted it back, desperately. And it was that desperation that had enabled her, just barely, to stay away. To want anyone or anything so terribly much was to invite dependency and Eva knew she was dangerously close to reaching that point.

Scary stuff. She'd learned the hard way not to depend on anyone or anything but herself and yet, here she was, falling fast and furious. And for what? A hologram! Assuming that's what Urich really was. The substitute program didn't work half the time and the other half, it was a mess.

She was a mess. Was she losing her mind? Or was she just finding it, discovering how severely she'd limited herself when there were awesome powers to be had, there for the taking, just by tapping into a neglected region of the brain?

Mind over matter. The book resting heavily in her lap claimed that the power to control objects with the mind—psychokinesis—was something everyone possessed, but that like telepathy, few knew how to access it. It was along the same lines as Einstein's claim that humans used only a fraction of the brain's potential.

Her own brain felt like mush. So did the rest of her. She couldn't eat. Sleep was an exercise in exhaustion, her dreams riddled with fantasies gone berserk. They were of Urich, of course. Urich. *Urich. URICH.*

He was like a song she couldn't get out of her head, a mythical god ruling supreme from the dias of her every need, fulfillment incarnate if she would only fall under his gaze and see forever in his eyes.

Going to the mirror, she saw that her own eyes shone with feverish anticipation. She put lipstick to the lips that longed for his and brushed the hair she wanted to feel his hands tangled in. Eva admitted to herself that were he the devil himself, she would surely jump into hell's fire for his searing embrace.

"Lady, beware," she said to her reflection. "Lady, beware."

5

URICH SENSED the caution in her; the elusiveness he had falsely spoken of to Raven was now there.

There, in her reserved greeting. There, in the her eyes' avoidance of his. But most of all it was in the guardedness of her mind, a shield of protective defenses raised against him.

He could sweep them away with the ease of a child knocking blocks to the floor. Although it was his duty to do so, he did not. Rather, he responded to her in kind, needing some protective defenses of his own.

"How have you been, Eva?" he politely responded.

"Great!" Seeing her smile, strained and overbright, he deemed her an abysmal liar. "How about you?"

Since he had no taste for lies, either, Urich raised an eyebrow as if he didn't qualify for such a question.

"So," she said, looking everywhere but at him, "what should we talk about?"

"Whatever you want." Her emotional distance, the evasiveness of her gaze distressed him, sparked a flare of anger at what stood between them. *Look at me*, he silently commanded. She did and he immediately regretted the connection he lacked the will to break.

"Okay," she said quietly, her eyes like a vast ocean of troubled water, beckoning him. "I want to talk about work, about an experiment."

Here it came, all her uncertainty over what he really was. More than anything, he simply wanted to tell her the truth and do away with this sham he well and truly despised. But duty decreed otherwise and no matter his feelings for Eva, he was sworn to propagate this hateful lie until she became a willing pawn in the master plan of his crippled nation, its future at stake and riding on her.

"You're disturbed." His commiserating tone was sincere—unlike the explanations he'd already prepared and she would be all too eager to accept, such was her human nature. "Why?"

"I'm very disturbed, Urich. And you're the reason why." She bit her bottom lip and he saw his own teeth raking their lush texture. Eva's breath caught and she pressed a finger to her lips. He saw himself teething that fingertip, sucking it into his mouth. She gasped softly and he struggled to withhold the images assaulting him, projecting into her.

"I disturb you," he said, his empathy great and wishing just as greatly to say she disturbed him even more.

"Yes. Yes, you do. You're not like the other experiment. The hologram I programmed to take your place isn't performing very well. And then there's you—a success beyond my wildest dreams. You make me feel and say, and—and maybe even do things I've never imagined before. Things I don't understand. Things that shouldn't be possible."

Perceiving she was about to touch him, Urich sent a warning command to her not to. Gone would be the illusion he had to maintain; gone would be his resistance to the touch he craved.

Her hand dropped to her side and she stared at him, her eyes too open, revealing all. She wanted to believe that the impossible was possible; and that made the convincing all too easy.

"Tell me, Eva, how long did it take you to create this program, otherwise known as me?"

"A year."

"And the other?"

"Half a day."

"Well, there you have it. The difference between what you threw together in half a day and what you created by pouring your heart and soul into me." And she had, more than she could possibly know. What he was doing, it wasn't right. He'd told himself, again and again, that he would do what he had to do. But now that he was here, he knew that to betray Eva, even for the sake of his people, was a crime he'd rather die than commit. Would they kill him for aborting the mission? Not likely. He was too valuable, an asset to be used, however they liked—but not for this.

Not for this.

As Eva nodded, clearly embracing his flimsy reasoning, no technology to support it, Urich could feel his heart hurting, physically hurting, while he braced himself for goodbye. And when he left, it had to be in the guise he'd come in. Where he came from and why, like himself, must remain secret.

The decision made, he carefully veered Eva toward this best and achingly difficult end.

"The other experiment is where your time should be spent, Eva. You can't duplicate the success you've had with me as long as you're neglecting your profession to indulge your personal needs. You could, of course, use me as you first planned, for experimental purposes." A logical option, only he wouldn't show up and she'd wear herself out trying to reclaim something that had never existed. That wasn't fair. How could he get her to put an end to this herself? *How could he leave without touching her—once, just once again?*

"I don't like that idea," she told him. "Professional success be damned, you're mine and I'm not willing to share."

"What you're saying just goes to show that you'd be better off without me." He willed her to believe it so, and so it was, but his own will was too weak to force her agreement. Seeking to persuade her, Urich firmly advised, "Send me away, Eva. Make it as though I've never been."

"I can't. I need you, Urich."

"No, you don't. All you need is yourself."

"Bullshit! I need to heal, learn to trust myself and others again. With you I've started to and—and don't you see how important you are to me?"

"Eva." He shook his head, denying what he had nourished to the detriment of them both. "Don't _you_ see the greatness of what you've done? You're an amazing woman who's been given a gift of genius. Your work is more than just that, because it's meant for the good of many. Find your fulfillment there and forget about me."

Following the path of her thoughts, he knew she wanted none of that. For too long the good of many had driven her and for once, what about her? _Her_, damn it. And why was he trying to convince her she had no further need of him when he couldn't be more wrong. But how right she was in refusing to argue, certain her logic would be no match against his.

How deftly her mind worked, concluding that her advantage was in the illogical, the heart. Knowing he couldn't compete with her there, Urich silently groaned.

"There's no joy or fulfillment in dreams or work or anything else when you can't share it with someone who cares. That's what we're always reaching for, Urich, trying to fill the hollowness inside. The hollowness that's inside everyone. Inside me. But when I'm with you, it's like being filled—with you, with all that I can be. How you do it, I don't know, but you do and I want more. More of you. More of me."

He commanded himself to be unmoved but it was a futile resistance. The plea in her voice touched him deeply, and moved the heart he'd thought incapable of feeling until Eva had brought it to life.

She made him feel more than alive, she made him feel too much. How could he leave and never see or touch her again? He was floundering in a tide of emotion, his every intention sucked under.

"You fill me as well, Eva," came his slow, irrevocable confession. "If it's more that you want, then—" *Don't! Give her what she wants and it's sure disaster.* Disaster already, every which way he turned. He was in a hole so deep there was no way to get out. With a sigh of defeat, Urich gave himself up to the grave he continued to dig. "Then more you'll have," he finished, unable to fight the images of intimacy that filled his thoughts and sealed their fates.

"Oh, Urich. I knew that you'd—" Eva stopped short. She felt a ripple of sensual suggestion, then it was gone.

Too fast to catch, but it had the effect of a catalyst. She suddenly found herself in a dark place where she feared to move. This was where she hid her secret fantasies, those desires that should be denied. But they were flooding out, rising against the dam of her inhibitions and demanding acknowledgement, appeasement.

Urich's gaze bored into hers and a flurry of other images rushed at her, flashing quickly and yet somehow lingering: wrapped in a rainbow, the touch of mink, scents of mist and musk, legs tangled, dark and pale, Beauty embraced by the Beast.

Her senses were reeling, and she was panting, all but hyperventilating in front of Urich. Urich, whose eyes were as glazed as surely as her own were, as if he were in the throes of the same blinding passion taking her over without a shred of reason or mercy to cling to.

Her lips began to pulse as if they were being kissed from the inside out, a kiss more intimate and complete than two mouths devouring each other could possibly devise.

It was nearly impossible to speak, even to ask, "Are... are you . . . kissing me?"

"Kissing, as I understand it, takes two—at least, for both to enjoy it." His cryptic reply was accompanied by the sensation of a blunt nail sliding down her spine.

"What are you doing to me?" Eva arched her back for more of whatever this marvelous thing was.

"The question is, what are you imagining that you want me to do?"

"I—Kissing me. Touching me. Urich, please, make it happen."

"Why don't you kiss me, touch me?"

"Because I can't. Or...I don't think I can and so I'm afraid to try."

"You tried before. And did."

Aroused. Dear Lord, she'd never been so aroused. Or so relieved, elated. "Then it really happened and I didn't just convince myself of what I wanted to be true?"

"You put your lips here." He fingered his neck, a savoring linger. "Mind over matter, Eva. It's like faith overcoming impossible odds. But nothing's impossible if you believe. You did it before. You can do it again."

A halting step forward and she was engulfed by waves of pulsing energy. Inhaling it, tasting, willing it to consume her doubts and fears, she claimed his force as her own.

Envisioning herself in his arms, Eva fell forward, wrapped her hands around—

His neck. He was there, his strong arms holding her. His lips, hot and moist against her temple, slid to her ear. "You feel like heaven," he said.

"I feel like I'm walking on water."

"You could do that, too," he assured her. "Or walk on coals without burning your feet. Anything you believe, you can do."

"What I believe is . . ."

"Tell me," he prompted, lifting her face to his.

"I believe if I don't kiss you I'll die."

"Death, like much of life, is an illusion."

"Urich?"

"Yes, Eva?"

"Kiss me."

6

DEATH. HE WAS SURELY courting his. The mission went beyond anything so simple as Eva's technological advances. They needed her mind, but only in the genetic scheme of things. Hitler had dreamed of creating a superior race, but his was a poisoned intent, unlike their own.

They had the male, but propagation was dependent on the woman selected as the perfect female specimen: Eva. She was reserved for a distinct purpose and no one, save the male, was to touch her in a sexual way.

And here he was, filling his hands with her hair, her face, sliding them hungrily over her back. Aborting the mission was cause to be stripped of rank, but claiming the means to their perfect race was the equivalent of treason, punishable by death according to law. If he wasn't found guilty of that, then Eva would likely kill him first with no more than a kiss.

She sucked the very breath of life from his lips, only to sustain him with hers. It wasn't a fair exchange, but he was too greedy to deny himself the better bargain.

She gave her mouth to him, freely, withholding nothing. And he took it all: the soft, moist interior plundered by his searching tongue. The slickness of her teeth parting their guard and allowing him to explore every secret of her mouth.

He knew of her secrets, the desires she feared to express even to herself. They were exotic, fascinating.

And enormously arousing.

They were sapping the control he was in danger of losing. His reason was deserting him, as well, lost somewhere in their kiss. Her mouth was a warm, encasing womb, breeding his need to mate with more than tongues and minds. *Deeper*, she was urgently, silently pleading.

So deep he went. The sound of her mewling whimpers called to the beast surging inside him, straining against the leash of his slipping hold.

You'll savage her, you know that you will. This is your way, but it's not hers. Focus. Focus on Eva. Hear her.

What he heard was the rustle of sheets, the flare of candle flames, the slide of a nightgown in satin. She was imagining him taking her in a manner far different from that of his own primal urgings.

But then her urgings shifted, the sinuous flow of their lovemaking giving way to a primitive awakening. Urich responded before he could command himself not to. With one hand on her hip, he snared in his fingers in the waistband of her skirt, jerked it down, rending the fabric and giving him access to the soft flesh he seized.

His other hand twisted in her hair, binding his wrist and securing his hold over her throat thus exposed. Pulling his head back, he fixed her with the ferocity of his gaze.

Eva was transfixed, unable to move, she was so stunned. Her excitement intensified even as apprehension took hold. Urich was looking at her as though he were a starved animal about to devour a meal alive.

She was that meal. And they were all alone.

He made that beastly sound again and her apprehension became a shudder of fright.

"Why—why are you looking at me like that? And what is that strange sound you're making?"

Silence. It pulsed like the beat of a war drum. A stalking announcement to precede a savage attack.

"Submit to me and open your legs."

Her heart rose to the throat he was eyeing and her stomach bottomed out. No romance, no foreplay beyond a mind-bending kiss? Not even a token seduction?

Her fear bowed to a swift outrage.

"I don't submit to anyone and I most certainly will *not* open my legs."

"But if you don't, I—I don't know what I'll do. I need what's between them, need it too much. *Give to me.*"

"What is between them is mine and I have no intentions of sharing it with you!" Her glare packed the punch of a knee to his groin.

Urich blinked. Once. Twice. That click-click computer-like assimilation that seemed the only normal thing about him.

He released her hair.

The drum slowed its beat, fading until the silence was as absolute as the void.

Eva glanced at his hand still clenched into her bared hip. What had initially excited her caused her to wince.

"Let go."

He did. So fast she couldn't track the movement. Lord, David Copperfield and Houdini combined couldn't pull a sleight of hand that quick. How Urich did it was yet another piece to the puzzle he was.

Puzzle be damned. She was so angry she wanted to slap him. And then she wanted to cry. He had turned something wonderful into a crude, ugly blow.

"You tore my skirt," she accused.

He bowed to her. "I'm sorry, Eva."

"Sorry doesn't get it, you—you...animal! That's what you sounded like and it's how you looked at me, too. And as if that wasn't bad enough, you had the gall to tell me to open my legs like I was some kind of cheap sex toy you picked up to get your rocks off!" The pain of it all caused her throat to tighten. She refused to cry. Later she would cry, but the hell if she'd let the reason for it see.

He seemed to see anyway. The remorse in his eyes was vast, entreating her as he reached to cup her cheek.

Eva jerked away. "Don't touch me."

"Please. Please, Eva, don't shun me for something I couldn't control."

"I'll say you were out of control. C'mon, Urich, let's hear them. Excuses. Surely you have some."

"All I have is the truth." He paused as if trying to put it into terms she could understand. A feathery brush to her cheek felt like the fingertips he'd clenched into a fist. "You were wanting me. All of me. And all of me responded to you, even the animal that you called to. There's one of those in you as well, but you've mastered it with a lifetime of denial. What you created in me went beyond desire, beyond description— something too strong and too savage to stop. Forgive me if you can. I never want to hurt you, Eva."

His words rang of truth, with a sincerity she couldn't doubt. She was still upset but Urich was closer to distressed. Miserable, in fact. And why? Because she'd gotten him so hot that he'd lost the control he usually had over her.

It seemed the "dry goods" weren't as unappetizing as John had convinced her they were. Urich had wanted to eat her alive and she couldn't deny that it held a frightful appeal. And she was kind of flattered—in a peculiar sort of way.

Not that she was up for a repeat performance, but she was too needful of this newfound allure to let it go.

Her smile a little shaky, she admitted, "If I'd understood the reason for your behavior, maybe I would have lost a little control myself." And what would have happened if she had? The idea of them going after each other like wild things was the kind of fantasy one kept behind that gate where all things libidinous resided—an ominous realm. Perhaps that was why she'd been so disturbed by those crude lyrics that had provoked an image which smacked of the forbidden. *The forbidden.* It wasn't a comfortable place for a woman who had been raised on the merits of denial. A lifetime of it.

"So, you really think there's an animal in me, too?" Eva asked.

"I'm sure of it."

"I want to know more."

He studied her for a while.

"The problem is, you lack self-knowledge," he said. "Ignorance breeds fear. Fear eradicates power, just as belief accesses it. You're very brave, Eva, but not without fear. It holds you back from tapping the force at your core. Call the force your potential, whatever makes you *you*—what you are and *can be.* The 'can be,' it's . . . well, it's like a fierce creature, a lioness you've trapped with this need of yours for control. Let her loose. She's the core of your strength, your unrealized potential. Fear, especially of failure, that's what keeps you from becoming all you can be."

The lioness—the bold, triumphant woman who embraced the night sky—she saw her again. But this time Eva heard her, as well—lips parted, mouth open, releasing a majestic, shattering cry.

The cry of the wild. The sound Urich had made. This time, her own. A ferocious feline cascade to his savage growl.

It gave her the shivers. But those shivers were no contest against the lure of risking a brief embrace of the lioness she could feel scratching to get out.

In that embrace, Eva found she was woman. Everywoman. Strong enough to be soft; wise enough to listen to a foolish heart. A heart that could laugh joyously and hold an ocean of tears. Her love was infinitely gentle and just as lethal. That of a creature who would kill to protect her loved ones. She was earthy and sensual. A spiritual being. An eternal mystery to everyman.

"You've seen her." Urich's tone was reverent.

"Yes," Eva said, her voice hushed. She felt as though she had entered a sacred temple and that temple was her soul. But what of her soul mate's? "I want to see you now."

He laughed quietly, seductively. "Yin to yang, Eva. Water to fire. Sheath to sword."

"Opponent to ally," she whispered.

Urich frowned at that. But then he nodded and surprised her by saying, "You're right. In all worthy matches, a pitting of wiles and wills is necessary to discover who's the stronger and ultimately leads."

How archaic to put the battle of the sexes into such terms. Eva started to point out that men and women were supposed to be equals. But some gene that had to be traced to the beginnings of time insisted otherwise, that Urich spoke the unvarnished truth. As did the wildish woman, the lioness.

The mating dance of nature. It was as old as Eden and no degree of civilization could alter its fundamental hold.

It seized her now. Eva looked Urich up and down, assessing this yang to her yin. A worthy match indeed. She tossed the gauntlet with a single slide of her finger over his chest. When he tried to capture her hand, she withdrew and issued the first challenge.

"I can't help but wonder what's under that shirt." With an aggressiveness that amazed her, delighted her, she said, "Take it off." *I am woman, hear me roar.*

Urich raised a lofty brow and with a confident smile, grasped the second-skin material. Slowly peeled.

Dear God. He was gorgeous, a bronze study in massive, symmetrical perfection. But what truly stole her breath was the dusting of what was too fine and silky to qualify for hair. She likened it to mink sweeping over his chest, narrowing from there to his blocked stomach, gathering density in descent. The pattern was like an arrow pointing below the waist of his pants, a tempting indicator to sneak a peek at the hidden destination of that sumptuous fur.

He casually tossed the shirt at her feet. It was a gracious, cocky gesture that he followed with a neat bow—one that implied he was at her service while accepting the accolades he was certain his body deserved.

Much as she hated to admit it, there was something damn sexy about his display.

"Your turn."

"My turn! You don't think I'm actually about to—"

"All right. Like you said, your body is yours and I'll respect it as such." He bent to retrieve his shirt.

Eva's foot came down on it. "I want you to leave it off."

"But it's not an even exchange," he informed her. "I exposed myself but you don't want to do the same. Fair's fair, so I'll return us to our equal state of clothing."

Spoken like a computer with the strategy of a cunning man. *You show me yours and I'll show you mine*, was that it? Urich was smiling now, smugly, letting her know he'd won because he'd shown her his and she had chickened out.

"Breasts are different," she reasoned.

"Yes," he concurred, eyeing the breasts in question. "Let go of my shirt so our differences aren't so obvious."

She couldn't let him win. She'd let John win, then nursed her wounds by suffocating what was left of her feminine ego. It was her ego gasping for life again, telling her she had pretty breasts and they deserved to be flaunted with pride.

Right under Urich's aquiline nose.

Eva called to the lioness and felt a surge of confidence there for the taking. A lick of her lips and there went the first button.

Urich's smile thinned, she noted with satisfaction. Her satisfaction grew with each button released. By the time she dropped her shirt beside his, Urich's lips were straining against teeth that surely wanted to take a bite.

At the moment, she'd rather like that. But even more, she wanted him to grind them in frustration.

"The other." He indicated her bra. "Let me see, Eva," he said thickly. "Let me see your breasts."

His gaze riveted on them, they grew warmer than they already were, began to pulse with that same savage drumbeat.

Her heart matched its pace. She was losing her nerve.

Uncountable times she had taken off her bra in front of John—her only lover, regrettably—and had managed okay. But now, when she wanted to be the epitome of self-assured finesse, she was all thumbs and fumbling fingers, unable to get the stupid hooks undone.

A sob of defeat was in her throat when Urich laid his palms on her shoulders.

"What I see is wonderful, just the way you are. There's no need for you to do this—not for me."

"But I need to do it for me." And then she saw his understanding, the strength of his belief in her.

She believed in herself. It was as close to ruling the sky as anyone could get, she realized with a flash of insight. No harder victory was won than defeating self-doubt.

Claiming a sweet triumph, she easily parted the hooks and slipped off a strap. With confidence and pride, she revealed a single breast. Urich didn't look at it. His gaze was on her face; his own conveyed admiration and open desire.

Eva wanted the bra gone. But her impatient grasp of the last strap was stayed by deft fingers lacing with hers.

"It's good to be strong by yourself," he murmured. "But it's even better to be strong together."

Eva knew she could do it alone, and that knowledge was enough. She guided the strap but allowed Urich to set a leisurely pace, his blunt nails tracing a path down her arm and making the rest of her quicken, quiver. *Melt.*

Together they dropped her bra and all the uncertainties it represented to the floor.

"I want you to look at my breasts, Urich."

"I don't know if I dare. They'll tempt me."

"I certainly hope so."

Slowly, so slowly it was a languid torture, he lowered his gaze. She felt the touch of it as if he were learning every detail of her skin with the fingertips he had elsewhere on her—skating up her sides, rounding over each breast, circles that grew smaller and smaller until his thumbs pressed the taut beads of her nipples.

The feel of him cupping her breasts, lifting, then consuming them with no less than awe in his gaze... Heaven help her, she was more than melting. Eva latched onto his waist before she liquefied into a pool of ecstasy at his feet.

"Ahh," he breathed. "Never, *never* have I seen or touched anything to rival the beauty of this."

Pretty as her breasts were, they weren't Silicon Valley perfect. But Urich thought they were the most beautiful things he had ever seen. And then she remembered.

They were the only breasts he'd ever seen.

Eva wished she hadn't remembered.

"I'm glad you like them, Urich."

"You don't sound glad."

Damn, he got her every time. "I am. It's just that... well... you don't have any comparisons to draw from."

"And you think this dilutes my opinion?" He shook his head and continued to stare at her breasts as if they were Mecca to a holy pilgrim.

"It can't—can't help but—" Lord, she could hardly form a coherent sentence. The way he was looking at her made her want to scratch her way down his chest and claw off his pants. How dangerously close she was to letting loose that animal rattling the cage of her lifelong denial.

Steadying herself, Eva put her hands to his chest. Her fingers sank into a texture so luxurious, so velvety rich that she would have wrapped herself in it if she could, wantonly wallowing in the texture of his skin. It was butter smooth, as warm as a hot toddy and just as intoxicating.

The lioness was getting stronger. Too strong. Unfurling inside her with such power and ferocity, Eva knew she couldn't handle, much less master, this untamed creature. Not yet.

Forcing her hands away, she said as evenly as she was able, "The—the fact of the 'matter' is, Urich . . . well, as—as incredible as you are, our relationship is—"

"Priceless." A pronouncement that refused debate.

"Oh, yes, yes, it is," she hastened to assure him. "But unfortunately, *very* unfortunately, it's limited."

"There aren't any limitations except those we place upon ourselves. Don't limit us, Eva."

"It's not me limiting us," she explained. His expression implied any perceived limitations were hers and hers alone. "What you have to understand, Urich, is that this chamber defines the parameters of our relationship. We don't exist outside of it."

"I exist. You're touching me, aren't you?" Urich grasped her hand and pulled it around his neck. His mouth lowered to hers, veered to her cheek. His lips grazed it, then his teeth nipped an earlobe.

"This is real, Eva," he whispered, his breath hot and tickling more than her ear. "It's as real as your feelings for me. As real as mine are for you. If you have any doubt how real you make me feel . . ." Sliding her hand down, he led her to cup what his pants were straining to contain. "Touch me, just like this, until you're amply convinced."

"Amply" was an understatement.

The temptation was great to delve past fabric and fondle what promised to be more than a handful. But one temptation would surely lead to another, and although she'd made great strides tonight, she wasn't up for that ultimate leap.

Urich was breathing hard, grinding his teeth while she lightly palmed him and did some heavy breathing of her own. Eva told herself the day would come when she would claim victory over everything that restrained her now.

She forced her hand away. "I'm convinced."

"Good," he said on a groan. His gaze turned inward and he seemed to be collecting himself while she hugged her arms to keep her hands off his chest and more. Especially more.

A minute or so passed before he blew out a "*whew*" then bluntly asked, "Do you want me, Eva?"

"I want you too much, Urich."

"Then want me enough to quit confining us to this place. Let me go with you, away from here."

A thought came to her, an absolutely crazy thought from out of nowhere, but there it was, insisting that she consider it.

"It's not possible, or at least it shouldn't be, but . . . I wonder if you might actually be able to exist outside the chamber." Not a chance, reason insisted. Eva rubbed her forehead, wanted to bang it against the limiting walls. "Forget that idea. It's—"

"Brilliant. Let's go."

"No!" Resisting his tug toward the exit, she dug in her heels and refused to budge. "We're not going anywhere, Urich. You require enormous amounts of energy to exist in any state, and the source of it can only reach so far. I'm sorry, but I just can't bear the thought of seeing you disintegrate while all I can do is watch. You're real to me here, and being forced to accept that you're not—that's one heartbreak I don't need."

"But you do need us," he argued. When she stubbornly held her ground, no more willing to argue than to move, he let it go with a shrug and a smile that qualified as crafty.

"Then so be it—for now. I won't force your decision." He said it as if he could but was generous enough not to. "But promise me that you'll think about this."

"I will." And she would. Later, when she was alone and Urich wasn't scrambling her emotions, making her mind jump through hoops, and sending her famished hormones into a frenzy.

"You'll think better without me. The sooner I go, the sooner you can get to your thinking."

"But I don't want to say goodbye."

"I'm always with you, Eva. Haven't you sensed it?"

There it was, the itch she hadn't been able to scratch that had become a distinct presence. She cocked her head, contemplating him. "Do you really watch over me when you're not—I hate to say this, but—activated?"

He smiled like a cat stealing cream.

"Urich, you are beyond comprehension." Fairy dust, he must be made of it. Breathing him in, she felt high enough to fly. "What on earth are you?"

His smile broadened, a disarming, beguiling smile.

"An alien."

For the space of a heartbeat she almost believed him. But then he laughed, inducing her to play along with the joke.

"Sure you are, Urich, sure you are." Eva laughed, too, and waved at the optical illusion of stars. "And I'm some queen of the universe."

"You could be." He raised her hand and kissed it as though he were a gallant knight courting her favor.

With that parting gesture he retrieved his shirt.

The stars flickered. And Urich was gone.

7

"YOU DID *WHAT?*" Raven came out of his chair with a speed Urich hadn't seen him show in ages. "Urich, this is insanity!"

"I disagree. The chamber's too restrictive. Once she decides, as she will, to let me venture outside it, I can investigate the other surroundings."

"We've tried this before. A terrible failure."

"Mylar invited his own death by using poor judgment. My judgment is sound. And don't forget, Mylar didn't have the advantage that I do." *Eva*, he'd almost said. Catching the near slip, Urich dangled the carrot he knew Raven couldn't resist. "Dr. Campbell will take me into her home and once there, I can solidify the liaison of friendship we want to establish with her—a lot quicker than by continuing with these brief charades."

Cinching his win, Urich sent a nudge to direct Raven's thoughts—into his mind and out of his mouth.

"If you're willing to accept this risk...the information you could gather would be invaluable to us. And it would be highly accessible if you're headquartered in her home."

"Exactly. Trust me with this, Raven, and we'll succeed beyond our initial goal."

"You're ambitious. Perhaps too much so."

"As you've often said, I am my father's son."

Raven raised a warning finger. "You should speak to Zar of this. He may have some concerns about your potential loss to us. He has already lost so much, Urich."

"As we all have."

"Yes." Raven sighed heavily. "Be cautious. Danger comes in unexpected forms. Even Ethan could pose a threat."

"I pose a much greater threat to him. Or to any other who would interfere with my purpose."

Raven tapped his lips. "Even . . . Eva?"

Eva interfered now, filling his thoughts when he had to be keenly careful in executing his own desperate plan.

"She *is* the purpose," he said evenly against the rising tide of protectiveness. "At least, the beginning of it."

Raven paused a long moment. "She is the greatest danger to you."

Urich couldn't deny it. Eva had caused him to compromise principles and loyalties that had been unswerving. Treason. He hadn't committed it yet, but she was capable of driving him to it.

"I'm aware of this," he confessed.

"Then you're aware that mighty nations have fallen because a male allowed a female to rob him of reason and he then fell prey to hers." Urich's nod earned a grave warning. "You will be tempted, as I'm certain you have been already."

"Yes. She does tempt me. Amazingly so."

Raven's concern gave way to alarm. "You haven't—"

"*No*." But how he had wanted to. Even standing here with his life in the balance, he still did.

Of all the battles he had fought, Urich knew they would be as nothing against the war of his taking what was not his to possess. But like the limiting perimeters of the chamber he would soon trespass, he could push the envelope of their bonding.

It wouldn't be enough. Not nearly. Yet it would be more than most humans could possibly conceive.

THE *MOONLIGHT SONATA* flowed from Eva's fingers as she played it with a new fervor and intensity. With each passionate stroke of the piano keys, she banished the memory of a long ago time she had played it.

She'd been twelve, dressed in her Sunday best clothes at a recital. She'd frozen with stage fright and had knocked over the piano bench in her haste to escape, her humiliation complete. She could still remember her parents' look of mortification.

Pouncing upon the keys, Eva declared herself a prisoner no longer to that horrible moment of defeat. She ended with a flourish, pushed back the bench and rose with aplomb, gave a neat bow to the past and then to the piano.

"So there," she said to them both, sticking out her tongue. It was juvenile and she should feel silly, but Eva decided she felt good. Damn good.

Now all she had to do was clean out the rest of the garbage she didn't want to deal with and she'd feel great. *Gr-r-reat!* Leaving the room, she prowled the house that felt closer to a cage.

In the kitchen she sought comfort with ice cream. A spoonful and back it went. Next she ran half a tub of water before deciding a hot soak held no appeal. Neither did another evening spent in the study she holed up in to avoid the bedroom.

Confronting it with the same determination she had the piano, Eva glared at the bed.

"How could you do this to me, John?" As she tore off the sheets that smelled of sweat and sex and another woman's perfume, then flung them at him, he merely shrugged.

"Hey, you're the one who'd rather be married to a Disneyland dream than a man," he retorted nastily. "You've got no right to blame me for taking from someone else what you don't have to give." Pulling out a suitcase from under the bed, he took it to the dresser and dumped into it the contents of

his drawer. "We're over. You can have the house, and our lawyers can squabble over the rest."

He was leaving, really leaving. Making good on his threat to go shack up with the bitch she'd ordered out of their bed, out of their house—theirs, damn it! Eight years of marriage down the drain, just like that? Her fault, according to John. And maybe some of it was. A marriage counselor, that's what they needed, not a divorce.

"John, no. Give us another chance and I'll—"

"Quit the project? Turn your study into a nursery and trade that goddamn computer in for a baby?"

"Let's be reasonable about this. It doesn't have to be all or nothing—I'd never ask that of you. We can reach a compromise, can't we? I'll cut back on my hours so we can—"

"Spend more time in bed? Yeah, sounds like fun to me."

"I've never turned you away." She opened her arms in a plea to be held. If he wanted sex, she'd give it to him as she always did. That was the trade-off for the affection she really wanted. And how she needed a hug—a single word of love right now. Then they could talk and try to pull what was left of their marriage together.

"No, you've never turned me away," he conceded en route to the door. Turning there, bag in hand while her own hands dropped to her sides, he said coldly, *"But a corpse would be easier to turn on than you."*

"How can you be so cruel?" And how could she debase herself this way, trying to pull him to the bed that he wanted no more to do with than the wife he spurned with a shake of his head.

"Cruel? I'm being honest. You're stiff as a block of ice and just about as warm as frostbite...."

Eva chafed her arms, remembering. Their confrontation had gone from mean to hateful. A memory infinitely more horrible than her recital fiasco, it refused to release its tainted hold.

And yet last night, with Urich, she had come so very close to breaking the chains that bound her. She wanted to tell him about the self-doubts she harbored, those suffocating failures she was desperate to escape.

Urich would listen. He would understand. He would help her find the path to her freedom from what was and claim what she wanted to be.

He would pressure her for his own release.

As if she had it to give. Psychokinesis, indeed. She had about as much of that as telepathy, and no way could she turn into some kind of conjurer who could keep a hologram around with the powers of a mind that Einstein would envy.

Then there was the belief thing. If it truly was the key, as Urich insisted, then his existence would be wholly dependent on her. If her belief gave way to reason, wouldn't he then disappear? And what if he existed only in her mind's eye? Virtually real to her but invisible to everyone else?

That would land her in the nut ward real quick. Eva rubbed at her temples and groaned. *What was she going to do?* She was half crazed as it was to see him, to touch him, even if only in the realm of her mind.

Her yearning was a restless stalker. Eva threw open the balcony doors and stepped from her bedroom's cloying past and onto the small terrace.

The future beckoned her to reach for a dream. Dreams— so like the stars toward which she now raised her arms. They glittered, looking small enough to hold in her palm and press to her heart—if only she could reach high enough to claim one.

Or take to the sky, flying on fairy-dust wings.

Urich had made her believe in fairy dust again; in the beauty of the mysterious, the power of faith in things unseen.

I'm always with you, Eva.

She couldn't see him but . . . yes. Yes. She felt his presence around and in her, imparting that indescribable mingling of serenity and breath-stealing sensation.

"I know you're out there," she whispered. "Out there somewhere, waiting for me."

Let me see, Eva. Let me see your breasts.

They were the words he had said the night before and whether they were memory's seductive refrain or spoken in the present, Eva didn't know.

Nor did she care as she bared her breasts to the stars and lifted them in offering to a dream lover who guided her hands. *Her* hands. But *his* touch.

Only his touch could make her skin feel so pulsingly alive.

"Kiss them," she whispered, with a soft moan.

Which was followed by the sound of whimpering, the taste of salt tears, the smell of sex. She felt like an animal; fertile, in heat. A vision came suddenly.

She was running, running, her heart beating in time to her racing feet. From a predator. Overtaking her, taking her down. Urich. She was on her hands and knees; he was mounting her, his teeth bared, sinking them into her nape—

Her legs buckled. A sharp cry splintered from her throat and she clawed at the wood, her nails scraping the floor.

What was happening to her? She was jerking, jerking all over. Her body was out of control—contracting, then expanding until even her veins threatened to explode.

"I'm scared," she sobbed. "I'm scared."

Let go, Eva. You need this and nothing bad will happen. Trust me. Trust yourself and let . . . go.

God, she was afraid. Terrified of this thing consuming her; this thing that was the core of her most painful failure. But to bow to fear would be failure abetting failure. She had to be brave. She had to believe. She had to trust Urich, but most of all, herself.

Eva let go.

Her thighs parted wide, knees digging into the wood, palms slapping down to support her bucking hips. The feel of a finger swirled into wetness, her wetness, then slid all the way to her mouth.

Her mouth opened and her head fell back. A savage purr rippled from her throat in waves of primitive pleasure. And demand.

"Fill me. *Fill me.*"

She was suddenly encased in a trembling darkness, a force that wrapped around her as tightly as a cocoon. A sharp sensation, like a bite, clamped her nape and she was . . . paralyzed. Restrained from all movement, she was a vessel that could only accept what her body could scarcely contain as she was filled.

And in no human way. She was being taken with a completeness denied to man, fondled and kissed from the inside out until she was splitting apart at the seams. Shattered with a stunning fury that flung her like dust to the wind and scattered her fragments, blindingly bright, like a nova burning itself out.

Eva collapsed. She lay there, on the terrace, listening to herself mewl while she was held prisoner to a ravaging ecstasy.

Like a storm spending itself, it receded to a languorous trickle. And departed. Then silence. Only the thrum of her heart, the sound of her panting could Eva hear as instinctively she reached for the lover who had filled her with an intimacy so profound, she wanted to weep. And did. Her fingers clutched air and she was left with nothing. Nothing but herself.

Her self was not the same. Eva searched for the difference and found a sense of wholeness within. An alignment of all that composed her. She felt . . . complete.

"Urich," she whispered. "Urich."

A breeze brushed over her and it felt like fingertips skating her spine, a licking kiss to the small of her back.

And then all was still. The air. The night. Her.

Hand over hand on the iron railing, Eva pulled herself up. Her hands were shaking as she rubbed the back of her neck, slightly numb but prickling with the return of sensation.

Her balance returning as well, she lifted her gaze to the stars. "I know you're out there. Somewhere. Waiting for me."

What are you waiting for?

The question was her own. It joined a multitude of others she was too exhausted to contemplate. For now, it was easier to accept that something extraordinary had happened: She had let go. She had found freedom by relinquishing control. Her fear had been conquered; failure had fallen to courage. *Sheath to sword.*

Her body felt like a sheath indeed, plundered by steel swathed in velvet. Muscles twitching, she swiped up her discarded sweater and returned to the bedroom.

It looked different. As different as the tenderness of her breasts, the heavy ache between her thighs. She'd never experienced those things in this room. Neither had she stripped with sensual abandon in front of the vanity mirror that had always seemed to magnify her lack of it.

Vanity. It was hers as she took in the fine arch of her neck, the beauty of her breasts, waist slim and hips gently flaring, then sloping to her thighs, which she parted.

She stroked all that she saw, caressed each blessing of nature, delighting in even her flaws. This was her body to love and accept.

To share.

It was then that Eva realized she couldn't have shared what she did not possess.

She possessed herself now. With a finger to her cleft, she claimed the sweet knowledge that she was a sexual being. Released from the restraints that had bound her, she watched her hand delve for the proof of her climax.

It had been her first. Before tonight, even alone it had seemed that the harder she tried to let go, the more frantic she was to keep control. On the balcony she had found freedom from what she had clung to—her fear of failure ensuring that she would not succeed.

A failure no more, she reveled in that shattering, exquisite release as she lifted its evidence to the light.

Eva blinked. Then blinked again. And again.

Still disbelieving, she switched off the lamp.

"*Good Lord.*" Waving her hand back and forth, she could only liken what she saw to sparklers sweeping the dark.

Heart pounding, breath nonexistent, she put a finger to her tongue. It tasted . . . faintly sweet. Nutty, like . . . Amaretto? An Amaretto fizzie.

Snap, crackle, pop. It sounded like she had a bowl of Rice Krispies in her mouth!

Eva hit the lights and threw on her clothes at breakneck speed. By some miracle she reached her destination without getting a ticket. She didn't waste time selecting a setting or activating a hologram that wasn't, but marched directly to the chamber.

"Urich!" No answer. "Damn it, Urich, I know you can hear me. I want you to beam your buns down here now. *Now!*"

"I only answer to 'Companion.'"

His voice echoed from wall to wall, lightly teasing but firm in its demand. Rather than argue, Eva said just as firmly, "All right, then. Beam your buns down, *Companion*."

"Please?"

"Please."

"The magic word," he murmured in her ear.

Eva swung around and he caught her in his arms—a lover's embrace. She gripped his shoulders, unsure whether to shake him as hard as she was trembling or hold him with the intensity of her awe.

"I—I know what you are."

"Besides being absolutely enthralled with you, what am I?"

Eva fell into his looking-glass gaze and saw the truth of her shocking realization: "You *are* an alien."

8

"WELL, WHAT DO YOU think?"

Urich swept his gaze over the living room once more, noting that many objects seemed of no utilitarian value, but did possess an aesthetic quality.

"Over all, oddly appealing." He focused then on Eva, unquestionably the most appealing creature he had ever met. "But even pleasant as these surroundings are—" he searched for one of those nebulous phrases humans were so fond of using "—they can't hold a candle to you."

Glancing at one atop her piano, Urich pointed at the wick. It sparked, then leaped to life.

Her gasp was one of disconcertment rather than delight— yet another sign of the wariness in her. It rankled, being treated like a stranger after the bonds they had forged.

Urich reached for her and although she didn't resist him, neither was she responsive. He commanded himself not to crush her to him and obliterate the shock waves crashing through her. With effort, he calmly said, "I'm the same but you don't view me as such. Why not?"

"You're an alien."

"Yes, you've mentioned that—" he made a swift calculation "—twelve times. What does it matter?"

"What does it matter?" she repeated. "A lot! You zap yourself around when you don't feel like walking and cruise in a spaceship instead of a car."

"A rudimentary mode of transportation, but it does hold a certain charm."

"Uh-huh. Just like my computer. 'Crude but cute,' I believe were your words. And never mind that you can think faster than my crude-but-cute computer can compute."

"But I thought this would impress you." Unusual as this place was, it had nothing on Eva's behavior. If only she knew how much he was risking to be here, perhaps she'd show some understanding instead of emotionally deserting him when he needed her so much. But no, he couldn't reveal his true situation; and besides, her caring and affection should simply *be* as were his own for her. So he'd shown off a bit, but that was no reason to rebuff his advances, tender as his touch to her cheek was now. "I didn't mean to upset you."

"Oh, but you have. I'm as evolved as a fossil compared to you." She shook her head, over and over until his palm fell away while she muttered, "An alien, an alien . . ."

Fourteen. Seventeen. Twenty.

"We've established that fact," he said abruptly, his patience wearing thin with this minor detail she was putting between them. "Why should any human make such a 'big deal,' as you call it, over a visitor from somewhere besides Earth? For the heaven's sake, what sort of mentality would actually believe that in all the galaxies, this is the only planet with intelligent life? Or that if some other exists, then it has to be less advanced than your own and unable to make the same overtures of contact that your silly little rocket ships are too infantile to make. That's preposterous. And arrogant!"

Having had his say, Urich deemed this petty matter over with. "Now that we've got that settled, I want to hold you. Close, Eva."

"No." As she broke away, her distress was palpable and her voice bordered on shrill. "You must want something else from me. Why else would you go to such lengths to form a relationship with me?"

"It seems our relationship was more to your liking when you thought me a hologram."

"Holograms can't deceive people. You tricked me, Urich. Made me believe I had something over physics, that I had powers of—" She touched him, then gasped dramatically, "Mind over matter!"

"But you do have that power," he hastened to assure her. "And many, many more. All that I guided you to, that you discovered for yourself, was true. The only dishonesty was in disguising my origins. And that was essential."

Even as he said it, Urich knew he was guilty of a deeper secrecy. He abhorred it but she was no more ready for that ultimate revelation than he was to provide it. For now he had to simply be grateful that he'd bought time for them both— time he would use to seek a solution to their dilemma.

A dilemma of much greater magnitude than his current one. Her mind was in chaos; the only clear thought emerging was that he had deceived her for some ulterior motive— horribly true—and that his being an alien made even his touch suspect.

Not true. Urich stroked her shoulders, hating the way she shrank from him. "Tell me, would you have trusted me, allowed me into your home, if I had exposed myself for what I was from the start?" he quietly asked.

"Not likely," she admitted. "I wouldn't have believed you and then, if you'd convinced me . . . Okay, I probably would have freaked. Actually, I'm pretty damn close as it is."

"A very human reaction," he said with the sympathy of the true "companion" he was. "Your race has a tendency to fear what they don't understand. There's much I don't understand about you, especially your emotions, but I'm fascinated by everything I've been privileged to absorb."

"Ab-absorb?"

"Yes," he reluctantly confirmed. "You see, Eva, I come from a civilization of logicians, highly evolved, but limited in their emotional capacity. We Deducians weren't always this way, and some remnants of our basic nature do remain. In an effort to reclaim some of what we've lost, I entered your mind and took knowledge of your heart. It's infinitely more complex than the powers I shared with you in return."

Eva wanted to hear more but she'd already heard too much.

Absorbed. By an alien. Good God, she'd been mind-melded by an alien, who surely thought her hi-tech holodeck a Romper Room to his Star Trek world. Did they even have blood? Did they sleep, dream, eat, bathe? *Have sex?*

She shuddered. Liberating and incredible as it had been, just what had Urich done to her on the terrace?

Eva started laughing. Laughing, laughing, until tears ran from her eyes. She was hysterical, that's what she was. In a state of hysteria. And when she came out of it, she'd wake up. This was only a dream.

"It is *not* a dream." Urich's voice cut through her wild laughter like the snap of a hypnotist's fingers. "Calm down and stop your rabid thinking. The effect it's having on me is very unpleasant."

"Then get out!" Eva shook her head. She felt violated, subjected to a calmness he had commanded when she felt perfectly entitled to her every rabid thought.

Urich stared at her, puzzled. "My presence there helped you surpass your self-imposed limitations. Why you should suddenly resent it is beyond me."

"Has it occurred to you that I might want some privacy? The least you could do is go 'Knock, knock—may I get inside your head and rummage around your heart, just long enough to *absorb* your every emotion and thought?'"

"The flux and flow of your emotions intrigue me," he replied with a maddening composure. "As for the ones you've created in me, they're strong and unfamiliar, very difficult to analyze. I'm hoping to better understand them by observing this thing called human nature. Such data is invaluable to those who are expecting me to provide it. You'll lend your assistance, won't you? And I'll share my knowledge with you in exchange for your help," he pronounced with the finality of a done deal.

So, he wanted to understand human nature, did he? By golly, he'd asked for it. "Okay, Urich, stuff this into your memory bank: My emotions are mine to share or withhold as I wish. They're not something to barter and even if they were . . . well, vast as your knowledge surely is, it won't do you any good when it comes to feelings. They're instinctive and unique to each person. Besides, emotions don't make sense. If you don't believe me, feel free to come on in when I'm battling a case of PMS."

Urich regarded her at length, considering what Eva had said. The air fairly crackled with the flare of her emotions while his own were divided between longing for a consoling touch, a kind word, and an almost-frantic need for the logical. Yet human nature simply wasn't logical. If he was to live among humans, he had to emulate them, at least. But that was—what did they call it?—a cop-out.

Deciding to "go for it," Urich said with determination, "I want to try this your way. But first, let me make sure I have this straight. My intrusion makes you angry. It doesn't matter whether or not I'm hungry, *starved*, for what's inside you because it's not mine to take unless you willingly give it. Correct?"

"Yes, he can be taught!" Eva slapped her forehead.

For his being so advanced, she seemed to think he wasn't overly astute. Unfortunately, when it came to this terra incognita of hers, that was probably true. And since it was true, it wasn't logical to feel insulted. But he did. A good sign? Yes, he believed it was. Maybe he was developing some human nature of his own to go along with his emotional acquisitions. Still, he was hardly prepared for the new mission he'd assumed to sidetrack his impatient peers.

"You're right, Eva, I can be taught," he said without the defensiveness he felt. An argument wouldn't get him what he was after, but a sincere appeal for help most likely would. "The question is, how much more do I have to learn? Humanity is like a labyrinth I'm lost in and you're all I have for a guide. I can only hope you'll be generous enough, care enough, to help see me through. This mission is a dangerous venture for me."

"Dangerous? What do you mean, dangerous?" she asked in sudden alarm. "Is our atmosphere bad for your health? Or—if you're afraid I'm going to blow your cover, forget that idea. I'd never do anything that would put you at risk."

Hmm . . . More than her help, he'd managed to summon her protective instincts. But protection wasn't what he really wanted. He wanted a hug, a kiss, an endearment or two. These he could have without too much guilt for bending the rules. Even those stolen touches he was so needful of, were within reason. Human reason, that was. But more than that was a breach of honor, a sure kiss of death, and had to be absolutely, unequivocally denied.

For now, he would be content with a simple assurance. So he asked, "Then you still care for me?"

"Of course, I do!"

"But only a moment ago, you didn't seem to care for me at all. How can your feelings change so quickly?"

Read my mind. It's something I couldn't explain in a lifetime. That's what she was thinking, but beyond that, Urich refused to let himself listen. It was Eva's right to tell him what she wanted to tell him; that much he'd grasped.

"Let's just say I'm a woman and leave it at that," she finally replied. And then she did something wonderful, something that no Deducian would do. Her hand caught his and squeezed. "I'm sorry, Urich, really sorry for getting so beside myself and making you think I don't care about you. I do. Deeply. It's just that I'm adjusting. And I'm worried as hell about what kind of danger you could be in here."

"Your concern makes me feel . . ." How *did* he feel? And when would he quit trying to analyze these feelings that didn't make sense anyway? Or maybe some did. After all, she was hugging him now and it made perfect sense that he'd feel . . . "Fortunate. Happy. Warm. You're right, I do have to experience my own feelings and not rob you of yours. There's the danger I mentioned—the range of human emotion can be toxic to my breed. We sent an emissary once to find out if we could coexist in harmony with your kind. He didn't survive."

Eva held Urich tighter while she wondered wildly if their emissary had suffered a fate similar to those of beings in the campy sci-fi flicks from the fifties.

Urich chuckled. "No, that wasn't his fate." At her glare, he said, "Force of habit. Sorry."

"That's okay, you slipped. You slipped and I'm having a hard time handling all this." Eva let it go. Her head felt like a Hula Hoop and she was dizzy from the spin. "I need to sit down. But first, I need a drink. Brother, do I need one."

"Would you mind sharing your drink with me?"

"Urich, you can have my whole bar—which isn't much, and for once I wish it was stocked—and while you tell me more, I'll try to drink myself sober. Heaven knows, I don't feel anywhere near sober at the moment."

"Your feelings have an inordinate importance in all that you say and do," he observed as she made tracks to the small bar John had come to find inordinately important to visit before climbing into their unhappy bed.

Eva shut out the thought in case Urich "slipped" again. Hell, he probably already knew! Later. She'd deal with it later. Right now, she was having trouble enough hitting the center of the glass. Having managed her own three fingers of brandy in the snifter and just as many on the counter, she asked, "What would you like? It's either this or beer."

"I'll have what you're having."

Eva jumped. One second he was twenty feet away, the next he was breathing down her neck. "I wish you'd quit that. It's unnerving and my nerves are shot as it is."

"Obviously." He pointed to the bottle's sloshing misaim and there went the brandy, bingo! Center of the snifter. "The laws of gravity are not as indelible as you think."

"Obviously," Eva returned dryly.

Urich chuckled. "You made a joke. Another human quality we don't indulge in often. But should. We're much too humorless in comparison to you."

"In comparison to my mood, I'm sure your pals are a barrel of laughs." Bracing herself with a swig, she pounded her chest and wheezed out, "Okay, let's hear it. What happened to this guy who didn't survive? I take it he died."

"Eventually." Urich lifted his glass—manually, Eva noticed with relief as she sipped from hers. His own sip was followed by a jerk. "What a strange taste. And it works a strange effect on the taster."

"Maybe you shouldn't drink that."

"But how else can I get experience? It's a better learning than observation can provide, and this certainly seems to be a pleasant indulgence of man." He indulged himself with half the glass and after several more jerks, licked his lips while eyeing hers.

"Eventually," she repeated, returning them to a subject that seemed a lot safer than Urich's dreamy gaze dipping to her breasts. "What happened to him before he died?"

"To be exact, Mylar was put to death."

Urich was smiling, seductively. And he was leaning in, getting close, way too close to her mouth. Eva put her glass where his lips seemed to be headed.

"Put to death," she echoed, trying to ignore the hot-flash effect of his nearness. "Who did it?"

"We did, of course." At her horrified expression, he explained, "It was the most compassionate thing we could do. We are occasionally capable of compassion." Urich finished his drink and although he didn't jerk this time, the dreamy look in his eyes came closer to downright amorousness. "Be compassionate, Eva. I'm in torture now. Kiss me...*kiss me.*"

"After we finish this conversation." After she finished her drink. Then maybe another one. "This Mylar, what was so wrong with him that death was kind in comparison?"

"He was mad. Ravaged by insanity. The emotions he tried to assimilate proved more than he could endure. We retrieved him and did what we could to salvage his mind and body, but our efforts were futile."

"His body? What was the matter with his body?"

"Many things. He put his eyes out to drive away the visions. He attempted to cut out his heart."

"Cut out his heart!" This was appalling. Macabre. And yet Urich was all but crooning the words, making his nightmarish recounting sound like a Julio Iglesias love song. "Why in the world would he do such a thing?"

"In a rare moment of sanity, he said it was where he'd been most severely afflicted. That it was the core of where emotions were seated and he couldn't bear the pain of what he had taken into himself. Mylar was a hybrid—part empath. He neglected to shield himself from negative forces—such as hatred, violence, jealousy—and something of a war between good and evil tore him apart. So, we honored his service by granting him his wish that he be put to death."

Was it Urich's gaze or the brandy that was making her so feverishly warm? Eva undid a button and flapped open the neck of her blouse. The air against her skin was cool but thick with a scent that seemed to be emerging from Urich. A heady aroma, intoxicating.

Arousing.

Gravitating closer, inhaling what was working like a hormone high, she murmured, "That's a tragic story. Why didn't Mylar leave us before so much damage was done?"

"The same reason I'm here when logic dictates a safer space between us." Urich closed the distance and nuzzled her neck until she purred. Ah, pheromones, he thought with a heady vagueness; no female could resist nature's most potent scent. Human males should be so lucky as their animal-kingdom counterparts. And lucky him to be some of both—and more. How tempted he was to reveal himself in all his beastly magnificence, but even delightfully light-headed as he was, he knew better than that. Eva was calm now, so sweet and soft in his arms, as supple as his murmured, "A woman was why he stayed."

"Then why didn't Mylar take her with him? Any woman who loves a man would do anything, go anywhere, to stay together."

"Love," Urich whispered. "It's like a virus in the veins, the mind, the heart."

"Feel my heart beat." She pressed her chest to his, swept her breasts against him. "It beats for you. Urich, I think I'm falling in love."

"Eva . . . Eva." His groan was heavy with the effort to sub-due the primal growl her words of love incited. "I fear that I could become a victim of this illness of yours."

"But it's not an illness. Falling in love is a wonderful thing. Even when it's horrible, it's wonderful."

"I've never been 'in love.' Does it hurt?"

"Sometimes," she whispered, looping her arms around his neck. "It hurts when your love isn't returned. And it hurts when it is. But that's a good hurt—feeling your heart so full that you want to cry with joy."

"To cry. . . with joy. Such a contradiction. I've never cried before," he confided between kisses. "Lips on lips and tongues stroking tongues, I've never experienced anything like it. It's too wonderful to even describe." His palm to her breast, he gently squeezed, savored the stolen touch that called to the beast who lightly pawed at her breast. "How did I ever live without this? Eva, what do you do to me?"

"I can only hope it's half of what you're doing to me," she moaned, urging his other hand to her belly. "You make me ache. Can you hear my womb crying for you?"

"Yes," he said in a hush as the scent of her arousal aug-mented his own—strong, so strong. How precariously close he was to being overtaken by those animal instincts from which he had sworn to protect them both. Hard as it was to think, he grasped a thread of reason and reminded himself, aloud, "This is your temple. Your sacred woman-place."

"Be there," she pleaded. *"Make love to me."*

She tried to slip her hand inside his pants. Feeling as if he'd just slammed into wall and had some sense knocked back into his head, Urich gripped her wrist, frantic to make her stop before she unleashed more than his gender.

"I don't know how to make love." His voice was terse with anger—anger at himself. How could he have let this go so far, instinct all but trampling intellect? He had to center himself, hold fast to those origins that were his only defense against this blinding urge to mate. Haltingly, he explained, "Making love isn't our way."

"Then take me your way."

Sweat beaded his brow and Urich swiped at it as he willed his mind to clear, as well. The haze was lifting, and with it came his silent gratitude for the ability to once again think past immediate gratification and to the consequences of it.

"It's sacred and it's savage. I'm sorry, Eva, I cannot."

"Then I'll teach you how to make love like a man."

Knowing how desperately he wanted just that, he thrust himself away and glanced warily at the bottle. "I never should have consumed this—this aphrodisiac. The effects linger, but fortunately for us both, I'm regaining control."

Her feverish hands racing over his chest, she demanded, "Take off your shirt, Urich. Lose your damn control and take me like an animal, a man. Take me the way you did on the terrace until we're nothing but ashes on the wind."

He gave her a small shake. "What I gave you on the terrace was little more than a caress, an affectionate kiss within. You needed release, acceptance of that part of yourself, and I was honored to be the means of it. But it was only a kiss. See?" He spat into his palm and held out the same glowing substance that had been inside her.

Eva swept his wet palm over her breast as if it were the substance of emotion. "You're very generous, Urich. Let me be generous in return and give you release."

His eyes lifted to heaven. With a deep, ragged breath he said, "I'm not as generous as you think. What I did wasn't just for you—it was for me, too. I was impatient and wanted to prompt your awareness so you'd take me in right away. Even now while I'm telling you 'no' when all I can think and *feel* is yes, yes, yes, I . . . I believe that I acted more with selfish need than wisdom."

"Be selfish." She enticed him with the wedge of her thigh between his. "Be needy. Be my lover."

"A lover? I can be many things to you, but never a lover as you know one." *Warn her, frighten her, do whatever it takes. Just stop this madness for both your sakes.* Grip stern on her wrist, Urich led it to his mouth, then lifted his upper lip to reveal incisors glistening with feral intent. She gasped as his teeth raked a needle path over the cushion of her palm. Turning it to her, Eva visibly paled at the sight of two thin streaks of scored flesh, rising in welts.

"You don't know what you're asking for," Urich said in a lethal whisper. He kissed her palm. Hard. Harder still was his warning gaze. "Much as you make me wish otherwise, Eva, I am *not* a man."

9

HE SURE COULD HAVE fooled her about not being a man. Two days on earth was all it had taken Urich to discover football, and now he was glued to the tube.

She hated football. The announcers were even more annoying than the fans working themselves into a frenzy over some big lug knocking his fellow lugs down and hugging an inflated piece of pigskin like a woman in bed.

Her own bed was too empty. Despite his warning, she had asked Urich to sleep, simply *sleep* with her. Although all she really wanted was to be held, he had said it would prove too tempting, then made a reference to some alien code of honor.

She didn't understand or like it, but things like honor deserved respect. And he did want her, no question, so she soothed her ego with that.

"Eva, come sit with me." He patted the couch and with a mischievous smile, Eva plopped onto his lap. Urich groaned. "Why do you keep torturing me like this?"

"Because it's fun. And because you deserve it for torturing me with this stupid football game."

"Rather barbaric, but there's too much strategy for it to qualify as stupidity. And it does seem to generate a good deal of excitement in the process of entertaining."

Urich was observing the fans intently, and when they went wild over a touchdown, he laughed heartily.

"You're really enjoying this, aren't you?"

A little sheepishly, he admitted, "Quite a bit, actually. It's not the sort of thing my kind approves of. Any form of combat is considered distasteful—except for debates. They can get fairly fierce, but our wars are restricted to words."

"So, besides these debates, what do you do for fun?"

Urich thought awhile about that. And then he grinned. "We aren't nearly as preoccupied with having 'fun' as you are. However, we do have something similar to a time machine when that occasional urge for a diversion strikes."

Eager to hear more, Eva asked, "What's it like? How does it work? Can you actually meet people from the past, go places in the future?"

Urich cut her off with a quick kiss.

"You're too tempting for your own good, much less mine," he grumbled. "As for your questions, let's just say that our resources are a millennium or two beyond yours."

Although he didn't intrude where he had promised not to, Urich knew what was coming next and felt the awful dread that was as close a companion as Eva.

"Will you take me there and let me try it out?" she eagerly asked.

"In time."

"Why not just zap us there now, then bring us back after we check it out?"

"Because..." *Once I take you there, they'll want to give you to the mate who's eagerly expecting your arrival.* Even the thought caused his stomach to twist around the strange food he had begun to acquire a taste for. His taste for Eva, a delicious morsel of humanity, was becoming an addiction. To give her up was unthinkable, impossible. It would destroy him.

Not to give her up was to invite a similar fate.

"Because why?" she pressed.

"You have to be cleared and I'm not scheduled to return until I have a report worth giving." A lie, a lie. He was scheduled to meet with Raven and Zar in twelve Earth hours.

And once there, he would lie, and lie again. For so loathing lies, he was producing them as though he couldn't lie enough.

"Well, seeing that you've been sent here to get a handle on humans and get some emotional experience under your belt . . ." She wiggled down and he endured a sweet agony. "Let's go out on the town. You've been taking notes from me since you got here, and I think you're ready to interact with the public at large. Besides, the sooner you go exploring, the sooner I can visit your place. I'll bet it's a trip."

"Yes, quite a trip." A one-way trip.

Her eyes, so open and trusting, searched his. "Why do I get the feeling that you're not nearly as eager to play host as I am to be a guest?"

"I think, Eva, that your expectations are other than what you'll encounter." At least that much was the truth.

"Don't tell me I'll meet a bunch of little green Martians and you'll turn into one, too, once you're back on your turf." Her laughter was a bubble filled with crystal bells. Urich relished it, cherished that bubble he could pop, those bells he could shatter with a revelation more horrible than any little green Martians could ever be.

"We're humanoid in form. And, like humans, our features vary with our genetic inheritance."

"So, are you considered a hunk there?" At his puzzlement, she said, "Good-looking. Handsome, attractive. The kind of guy women drool over."

Women. He was suddenly uncomfortable with more than the erection about to split open his jeans. After a steadying breath, he explained, "Physical attractiveness isn't any more important to us than the pursuit of frivolous pleasures."

"Wow! Just the kind of place that Cindy Crawford would hate and lots more of us would love. Eat as much chocolate as you want, forget about makeup, slouch around in your sweats? Hey, sounds good to me. Except for that lack of interest in frivolous pleasures, you could have millions of women begging Scotty to beam them aboard."

They didn't have Scotties and they didn't beam, but Urich refrained from making reference to that amusing "Star Trek" show, filled with more human insights than cosmic accuracy. Eva adored it with a passion to match the football zealots.

Focusing on the television in the hope Eva would drop this conversation, Urich watched a player fumble the ball. Observation was becoming less and less satisfying; how much more interesting to be in the game . . .

"Wait a minute," she said, blocking his view. "If looks aren't important, how come you seemed so . . . well, kind of arrogant, when I took one look at you and did some drooling myself. And then, when you took off your shirt and acted like a—" Eva pouted prettily as he gripped her hand, which was releasing a button on the shirt she'd bought for him the day before, along with a variety of other attire that he'd modeled while she lavished him with compliments he had delighted in.

"If you must know, I read your every drooling thought and since I'd never been viewed so wantonly before, I was very flattered and succumbed to a—an ego trip. Most illogical, but you have a maddening ability to interfere with that once-reigning portion of my brain. Now, hopefully, you'll preen over that while I concentrate on the game."

Peering around her, he shook his head. Another fumble. Urich narrowed his gaze on the ball slipping from hands trying desperately to keep it. Just as he was about to lend some assistance, Eva readjusted her position. Her legs straddling his, her soft behind riding his knees, her even softer breasts level with his vision, she sighed with pure pleasure.

"Genetic inheritance is really interesting. Lucky for me, I get my breasts from my mother's side of the family. Unfortunately, I get my hips from my dad's. Mom says they'll come in handy once I decide to have babies. She's always after me to find a decent man and get to it, since time's running out for me to supply all the grandbabies she wants."

"You want children," he said more tightly than the clutching of his heart, the fisting in his loins.

"Sure, I do. But finding a decent man who makes me feel as indecent as you do, isn't easy to come by."

This conversation was becoming more painful than his physical distress. Much more of this and he would have to put Eva to sleep before he did or said something irreparable.

His silence only served to make Eva more talkative. "The strong, silent type definitely holds some appeal. But they can be a little anal retentive, and that's a real turnoff. Mom says I'm too selective, but after John I decided, better no man than the wrong man."

"A smart decision."

"I think so. Otherwise I might have settled for less and spent my life regretting it. Life's too short for regrets. One thing's for sure—I don't regret bringing you here. The house used to seem so empty, filled with ghosts, but you've brought it to life. And you've brought *me* to life, Urich."

Although her words told him much, her eyes spoke volumes more, made him want to confess that he coveted the seeds of love that had taken root in her.

"Your home is like you, Eva. Warm, comforting, and full of fascinating contrasts." Realizing he was courting an intimacy they were both too needful of, Urich tweaked her nose—a playful gesture that made no sense but he found delightful all the same, particularly when she giggled. "Not so different from teams of athletic warriors working together against their opponents who're striving for the same goal...?"

"If I didn't know better, I'd think you were more interested in that boring game than me."

"Of course not— Touchdown!"

"My mother's a football widow. She copes with it by spending a lot of money while Dad swigs beer and divides his yells between 'Get your head in the game!' and 'Yes! Yes! Yes! Touchdown!' Actually, Urich, he could give you a few pointers on how to yell properly. As for the beer swigging . . . want one?"

"Extra point!"

"Guess not. Well, enough about me and my parents. What about yours? Which side of your family do you take after? Your mom's or your dad's?"

Damn, but she was tenacious. *Damn*. Deducians were provoked to profanity even more rarely than they laughed. And yet he had been driven to silently swear over a little thing, really. Then again, it was a sensitive subject for him.

Sensitive. Yet another human trait. It seemed he was fast becoming more human than not. He liked Earth food. He liked their clothes. He was entranced with this game Eva was competing with, making him frustrated with her interruptions while feeding his ego with her hunger for his attention.

Ego, a self-indulgence that Deducians didn't indulge. But there it was, his ego insisting he had no need to hide from Eva what was considered better ignored among his peers.

"I look most like my father—a Deducian, pure as they come. As for my mother, she came from another race known for their powers over minds and—" he allowed himself a small smile "—matter. I'm a hybrid, and that sets me even more apart than other Deducians—a very aloof breed. You'd call me a loner, I believe."

"I can relate to that."

"I know. It's one of the reasons I feel more aligned with you than anyone I've ever known before."

"Even your mother?"

"I never really knew her." There were so many things he would have to reveal to Eva; he'd lay the groundwork here. "She was extinguished shortly after I was born. The last of her kind, she was a sole survivor, discovered by my father, who to this day insists she manipulated his mind in order to be his mate. They only had one child. Me."

"You mean he didn't love her?"

"Even then, love was something rarely experienced. And those who did were pitied for such a loss of logic." Let them pity him; he pitied them for their deeper loss.

"That's awful. Please don't tell me it was your father who 'extinguished' your mother."

"Heavens, no. Though euthanasia's acceptable—Mylar for instance—murder just doesn't exist with us. My mother was a victim in a bloodless—but insidious—overtaking."

"Are you saying that she was a casualty of chemical warfare?"

"Something like that." Urich gazed longingly at Eva's breasts, then forced his eyes to the game he wished he could escape to. "Eva, please, there's less than ten seconds left, the teams are tied, and the Forty-Niners' time-out is almost over. Which do you want to win?"

"I don't care."

"Humor me."

"Only on a wager. I win and you drink a beer."

"I'll match those stakes. If I win, you let me watch the next game in peace while you go shopping."

"Deal," she said smugly. "I'll take San Francisco. The Packers can't intercept and score in ten seconds. The Forty-Niners have a chance at a field goal."

"I don't think so." Urich pointed to the ball, which flew from the quarterback and landed into a Packer's arms, his feet racing over seventy yards. Urich shouted, "Yes! Yes! Yes!

Touchdown!" at the sound of the buzzer and the cacophonous roar of the crowd.

"You can't do that!"

"But I already did," he said with a grin.

"It's—it's not fair."

"Why not? It's only a stupid football game, remember?"

"Well, yeah, but—it's just not fair."

"As you Earthlings say, all's fair in love and war. Actually, I'm beginning to like the way you humans think."

"I think you cheated."

"And I think you're a sore loser." Urich darted a tongue between her lips and while she was busy reeling from that, he said decisively, "Eva, I won."

10

"HOW AM I DOING so far?" Urich asked, squeezing Eva's hand beneath the small table as he scanned the Chinatown restaurant with more than his eyes.

"Great, just great," she assured him. "Except ... I don't mean to sound demanding, but when you're out with someone it's considered impolite to seem more interested in your surroundings than you are in being with them."

Unlike the game, he realized that her wish for his attention was more a subtle coaching in social protocol.

"You're a good and patient teacher," he said, his gaze warming on her. "You're also a sight more beautiful than anyone else here."

Eva glanced at the other woman he had been studying. "I do feel pretty, but—"

"Beautiful," he insisted.

"Okay, I feel beautiful. But that woman is absolutely gorgeous." Although Eva gave a smile, he saw the worry it belied. "There are millions of women who'd love to get their hands on you, Urich. You're bound to meet your share of them and ... and I'm afraid of losing you the way I lost John. Only it would be a thousand times worse."

He could tell her that when Deducians mated it was for life and infidelity was nonexistent. But such assurances were denied him and Urich felt a surge of rage at that. With difficulty he subdued the simmering anger that could shatter the room like a bomb should he vent it, and said with forced calm, "You could never lose me to another woman, Eva. In all the universe, there's not another like you."

"I'm glad you think so."

"It's more important for you to believe so," he reminded her. And then he confided, "I liked telling you that. You've been the one tutoring me lately and I'm starting to miss our little sessions in the chamber."

"So do I. Want to go there later?" Hopefully, she added, "Or maybe sneak into your time machine?"

"We don't need either one." He tapped his temple. "Your powers are as close as this. Let's give yours a try, shall we?" He glanced at the woman who had engendered Eva's ridiculous concern. "Open your mind and visualize a line, like a phone wire, running to hers."

Eva's expression of eager curiosity didn't mesh with the disapproving shake of her head. "I told you that's a no-no."

"Oh, come on, Eva. What's the harm in taking just a peek?" When she hesitated, he goaded her. "Why do I get the feeling that you're hiding behind morality because you're afraid you'll fail?"

"I've gotten past that," she haughtily informed him.

"Then prove it." With a sly smile, he added, "I'll help."

"I can do it by myself." She bit her lip as if wishing back the defensive retort her pride demanded she make good on.

He let Eva struggle past her self-doubts, then mentally lurch toward her target. Perceiving she was about to careen into the hyperactive child two tables over, he swiftly interceded to guide her telepathic trek.

"Oh. Oh, no." Eva clutched his hand and whispered urgently, "I want back. Get me back, Urich."

Seconds later she latched onto the glass of plum wine he didn't dare touch. But he wanted to. There were so many human things he wanted to indulge in—and plenty he didn't.

"Appearances can be deceiving, can't they?"

"I am so glad that I'm me instead of her."

"Sad, isn't it? Leaving home, certain physical beauty will lead to a movie career—empty promises made, then broken after she's been used. Used, then discarded."

"She wants to go home but she's too ashamed."

"Yes, just as she's too proud to return after lying about who she knows and how well she's doing. How odd that pride keeps her from those who really love her, while her lack of it is why she's here with that married producer who loves her no more than she can stand the thought of sleeping with 'the creep.' But she will. And she hates herself for it."

"The girl who left Iowa with stars in her eyes..." Eva sighed, sadly. "I feel sorry for her. Don't you?"

"I could." He gestured to the room of diners. "Just as I could feel pity or joy or hope for most everyone here. The vista of emotions around us is almost overwhelming—it's like an assault I have to shield myself from." He pressed his temples, blocking out the clamorous roar.

"Urich? Are you okay?"

"I have a monstrous headache." He managed a strained laugh and focused on Eva. She was his best defense, a calming balm. "Serves me right for paying more attention to my surroundings than the lady I'm lucky to be with." Funneling the tremors inside his head out and away, he heard glasses clanking, china trembling against metal.

A sudden crash nearby was followed by a torrent of angry epithets spewed upon the kneeling server as she hastened to clean up the mess of broken china and glass. Steam rose from the array of splattered food, surely burning her hands while she endured a stinging humiliation.

"That is so mean," Eva quietly seethed. "The poor woman probably works for pennies and scraps while that jerk lives off the profits of slave labor."

"He does." Compelled to stop the display of power's abuse of others, Urich stood.

"Where are you going?"

"To clean up the mess I'm responsible for."

"Urich, you're just going to get her in more trouble than she is already. It's better if you ignore what's going on."

"That's a pervasive attitude in your society and one I like no better than this ugliness I have no intentions of ignoring." With that, he stalked his way over.

"She is clumsy," the other man said, as if that excused his outburst and placed the blame justly.

"You're cruel." Urich perceived evil in the man. It was like a worm eating away his brain. While mentally purging himself, Urich dropped to his knees and caught the woman's scrambling fingers.

He touched her scalded palm. She gasped and her expression fluctuated from gratitude to fear. Fear of his healing; fear of the scowling observer.

Although a sweep of his hand could have put everything back together as it had been before she dropped it, Urich forced himself to lend his assistance as a human would.

Or at least, as a human *should*. His disappointment in the other diners gave way to growing approval as another pair of hands joined in. Eva's. And then she was joined by a child and his mother. Many more hands than were needed, but he took solace in what it symbolized.

The server thanked them profusely in broken English, yet the language of her heart was universal. Tears welled in her eyes. Searching them, Urich perceived the goodness in her; and she had not been treated well by life.

While the other diners, save Eva, returned to their seats, Urich claimed the tray.

Gone was the animated chatter in the restaurant. All eyes were watching: The server tugging at the tray he refused to give up. Urich towering over the little man who was contemplating his revenge once he had the woman alone.

"You're cruel," Urich said again. With a mental twist of his hands, the worm convulsed and its diseased owner's eyes bulged. "You owe her an apology. Do it."

As if seized by apoplexy, he sputtered, "S-s-sorry."

"And now, to the rest of us for spoiling our dinners with your distasteful behavior."

"Din-dinner's free."

Greedy as the bastard was, Urich knew he'd be hurting even more tomorrow than he was now. His brain was squirming, gasping for a malevolent breath.

"Take this." He shoved the tray into unwilling hands. Every instinct the man possessed rebelled. He lacked even a particle of sympathy or humility.

Urich decided a lesson in both were in order.

The man grabbed his crotch and there went the tray, *bang*, to the floor. He scratched, scratched furiously with both hands while he hopped from one foot to another, his polished shoes slipping and sliding among noodles and sauce, reminding Urich of a "This is your brain" commercial he had seen.

He discreetly held out an empty palm, closed and then opened it to reveal a fortune cookie. Cracking the brittle shell, he read the message planted within: "Confucius say, 'He who treat other like dog will be thrown like bone to wolves.'"

His grin ominous, he snapped his wolverine incisors, then tucked the message into its recipient's pocket. Hands divided between furious scratching and flailing as if warding off the evil eye, the man hippity-hopped backward and disappeared through the swinging doors.

A thud and a yell were proof enough that the doors had smacked him in the face as directed. Satisfied, Urich turned to the roomful of speechless diners.

"Ants in his pants," he explained.

A snicker was followed by a chuckle and then guffaws of laughter. He hooked his arm around Eva's shoulders and they left, the sound of clapping trailing them out to the street.

She nuzzled close as they walked aimlessly, giggling for an entire block before she asked, "Did you really put ants in his pants?"

"Just the sensation of them, a vivid image in his mind, and ample welts to remind him of his lesson."

"I hope he doesn't take it out on that poor woman."

"He won't. I made sure of it."

Stalling him beside a curio shop she anxiously whispered, "What did you do . . . besides ants and magic cookies?"

"Let's just say that I impressed on him that if he wants to keep the bone in his pants, then he'll treat her kindly. She'll be receiving a generous boost in her salary in order to support the child she's been struggling to feed."

"Urich, Urich." Eva sighed. "I don't know whether to hug you to pieces or lecture you on playing God."

"I'm not a deity and I would never wish to take that weight on my shoulders." Too much weight there already, he longed to unburden himself on her. "Hug me to pieces," he told her, needing that human comfort.

Hug him she did, tighter than tight. He wanted to hold her and never let her go; but go soon he must—to meet with those who meant to take her from him. Gripping her, he was seized by more than his primal urgings. He wanted to make love to Eva, wanted to be a man. He wanted them to be bound by human vows and all else that was denied them.

He couldn't think of it; frustration engendered anger and he lacked mastery over such blinding emotions. Fearing he would snap her spine with the force of what he struggled to contain, Urich called upon the tenderness she summoned.

Love was as tender as his kiss and as heedless as her own. Kissing him, kissing him. Madly, completely, until he was consumed with the urge to tear off her clothes. It was the animal within that he battled now. It was the man he so wanted to become that harnessed the wolf and gently broke the kiss.

"You're a witch. A witchy woman who's got me under her spell. I'd give you the world if I could, Eva. As it is—" he gestured to a red silk shawl scrolled with a golden dragon displayed in the curio shop's front window "—I can't even buy you a gift. Maybe I should get a job. Now *that* would be an experience—a lucrative one."

"I have a better idea. You can help me out with my work. We'll be a team and that means I share my paycheck with you."

"But I'd give you anything for free. Even the means to converting matter."

"Much as I appreciate that tempting offer . . ." She shook her head. "I have to do it on my own. Discovery has to take its natural course, just like relationships, and it would be a mistake to get where I'm going before I'm ready to be there."

What a marvel she was. Urich nodded his understanding, his supreme approval. "You're very wise. Is it any wonder that I looked the universe over and didn't see a one who could compare with you."

"Huh?"

"Never mind," he said abruptly, going for the door. "Let's find a special something to celebrate the night. And my new job. I'll buy—against the wages I'll be earning."

As they roamed the store filled with aromas and objects and humanity, Urich wondered how he could ever leave this world, so different from his own. Deducia seemed more and more an alien nation that he did not belong in. Belonging—what an indescribable feeling it was. So many feelings he was experiencing. Simply watching Eva glance longingly at the shawl, he felt a quick stab of yearning for her. He wanted to possess her, shower her with every luxury in the store.

Money. He suddenly wanted a lot of it and he didn't want to take Eva's. Greed. Pride. Possessiveness. He definitely had the makings of a human with his share of flaws. Add that to the beast he could be, and Eva wouldn't have the energy to even look at another man.

One was looking at her now. *Jealousy.* Stanching the impulse to send the admirer flying through the store's window, Urich seized the shawl and draped it over Eva's shoulders.

"This is yours," he pronounced. Then, loudly enough for everyone in the store to hear, he said firmly, "And you're mine."

Eva flushed, looking both embarrassed and pleased with his proprietary announcement. Stroking the shawl, she whispered, "It feels almost as sinfully fine as your chest."

He wanted to tell her that if she thought his chest was "sinfully fine," the rest of him would be hell incarnate and she'd have more than the devil in her bed.

"I'll let you play with it tonight," he whispered back. When her gaze darted to his fly, he quickly drew the line above his belt. "With my chest, that is."

"Fair being fair, I'll let you do the same."

His eyes slid from her bosom to the neck he lightly stroked with his thumb. There was one way to stake his claim and protect her from the very reason he was here. . . .

A monumental decision—not to mention that Eva would have to agree. And what she would be agreeing to would take more courage and commitment than any human woman could imagine in her wildest dreams.

"I'm hungry," Urich said. "Let's go." Clamping an arm around her waist, he made for the register. But as they passed the man who had been admiring *his* woman, Urich discreetly bared his teeth in warning. That, coupled with Urich's ferocious glare, persuaded the man to take to the street.

At the counter, Eva rummaged in her purse. Before she found her wallet, Urich asserted, "This is my gift to you and that means I do the paying."

"But you don't have any—"

"Here's the money," he said, pulling a wad of bills from his pocket, then handing them to the clerk. Before Eva could protest, he said, "Keep the change."

"But sir, there must be a thousand dollars here and the shawl's only a hundred fifty."

"Would you like some more, Eva?" He waved at the store's entire contents. "Or anything else? Anything you want, anything at all, it's yours." He took her grinding jaw as a definite *no*. "In that case, we'll just take this. Come along, dear," he said, trotting her out before she made a scene to rival the one in the restaurant.

Once on the street, she flung the shawl at him. "I can't keep this! Take it back in, say I decided I didn't want it and get that counterfeit money back."

"But it's not counterfeit. I borrowed it from one of your government money-supply houses. I'll rematerialize it, once I've earned some of my own."

Hands on hips, Eva huffed, "That's not how it works. What you did was wrong, Urich."

"Wanting to give you a token of my affection is *not* wrong. Your rejecting it is. And that makes me feel . . . hurt. Yes. Hurt—that's what I'm feeling." And more, so much more. The blaze of her eyes, the scarlet color of her cheeks and lips worked like a stimulant. His system reacted, released the pheromones that attracted females and triggered their instincts to breed.

Eva sucked in a temper-charged breath. Suddenly, her senses were assaulted by that scent she couldn't resist. Urich smiled knowingly as she leaned in, struggling to stay angry and losing the battle before it was started.

"You . . . you really shouldn't have borrowed that money. Promise you won't do it again?"

"Only if you accept my gift and thank me with a kiss."

She latched onto his neck and was about to kiss him like mad when another woman passed by, stopped in her tracks, then turned.

Eva watched as the woman all but slithered her way over. She was joined by several more, all of them moving in, threatening to edge her out. Her reaction was immediate. She pushed Urich away from her rivals and hissed.

The hiss was still sliding through her teeth when Urich said, "Uh-oh," grabbed her from behind, and with a snap of his fingers, got them out before she started clawing.

A second later, the sound of lapping waves and distant laughter from Fisherman's Wharf blended with his sigh of relief.

"Sorry, Eva. We'll stay by the bay until my hormones reach a safe level. It shouldn't be long, after that scare." Pulling the shawl around her, he laughed as though he'd gotten a charge out of her primal show of ownership.

"I—I was ready to claw their eyes out," she gasped. His scent was indeed fading and she glad for it. "What *is* that?"

"Nature's perfume." He ran a blunt nail up the side of her neck. "It's what male animals emit to lure a female."

"Well, you don't have to emit anything to lure me and I'd rather not feel like such an animal again myself."

"I'd rather that you did," he said into her ear. A nip of her lobe and she felt his teeth rake a light path over her jugular. "The animal within, Eva. Nurture her. She's your strength and you'll need her to survive the animal in me."

11

SHE SAW THEM ONCE MORE in the chamber, remembered how ferociously he'd reacted to their first kiss. Urich's first kiss ever; amazing as that was, it surely had nothing on "his way" of getting cozy in bed. *Just what did they do and with what did they do it?*

"Is that what you really are? An animal?" Eva asked.

He growled softly and instinctively she stepped back.

Urich sighed heavily. "We'll talk about it some other time." He swiped up a small stone and pitched it over the bay. It seemed to sail straight for the full moon illuminating the night.

"That's quite an arm you've got there." She patted it, hoping to restore their easy companionship. "Boy, would the Dodgers like to get their hands on you. You could pitch a fastball that'd blow a hole through the stands. Heck, I'll bet you could hit a homer to the stars."

"The stars." With a snort, he dismissed them. "I don't want to go back there."

She didn't want him to go back there without her. To actually think of traveling through space, exploring brave new worlds, new civilizations, to boldly go where no man had gone before— Whoa! "Star Trek," move over!

"Where is your other home?" she asked eagerly.

His hand slid over hers and he led her to point at the brightest glimmer riding high in the night. "Just past the North Star, over the envelope and into the black hole."

"Then there really is one!"

"Of course." Tilting her face to his, he smiled indulgently. "Your excitement is such a joy to me. In all my years, I've never been blessed with gifts like you give me."

So many gifts he'd given her, not even a thousand shawls could come close to an intangible one. She stroked the embroidered dragon that ran from shoulder to elbow and was reminded of Urich. Sleek and lethal, compelling in its fiery beauty, but seeming to hold the wisdom of the ages in its taloned grip. "Just how old are you?" she asked.

"In your linear measure of days and years, I'm close to ancient." Then he hastened to assure her, "But not very old in our parallel universe. Thirtysomething, like you."

"You mean time's different there?"

"It's . . . how to explain this? While we live in our present, we can go exploring—backward, forward, sideways. I've seen my share of history."

"What about the future? Have you seen it?"

"Variations of what might be." His face clouded. "We create our destinies with the decisions we make. Even pure logicians aren't immune to changing their minds." Significantly, he added, "Or having them changed by a single, fateful meeting. The future, Eva, can and does change. That much we do have in common with Earth, despite our differences."

"And despite all our differences, you still found me. How?" *Why did you find me?* Eva didn't bother to ask yet again, knowing that he'd give her an answer that was there but not quite, pat and yet amorphous.

Into the air he drew the shape of a square, glowing lines bending with the wave of his hand. "Imagine a flexible window. I looked through it and there you were, close as a sideways step."

Eva passed her hand through the holographic image he had created without the single beam of a laser. "Amazing, absolutely amazing."

"Not nearly as amazing as you."

It was really just too much. Except for her IQ, she could have been Ms. Average USA —heck Ms. Average Earthling, for that matter.

"That's part of your allure," he murmured.

"Urich . . ." she said warningly.

He offered his wrist. "Slap it if you want to."

Slap it she did. Only to have him to slap hers back.

"Hey!" Shaking her stinging hand, Eva demanded, "What was that for?"

"Consider it a Deducian kiss. Just a peck, but I could go for a good one. C'mon, go at me." When she didn't move, he chuckled and said, "Here, I'll give you some incentive."

Incentive enough, he gave her a small push. Eva stumbled back, wobbly on the heels that buckled, then flat on her fanny she went. Urich laughed heartily, then laughed even harder when she crouched and lunged.

Throwing her weight against the chest he slapped in invitation, Eva took him on. He hit ground with enough force to qualify for an earthquake tremor.

He caught her atop him and said with approval, "Very good. That's one helluva pucker you pack."

Flushed from the tussle, Eva panted, "Don't tell me this is how you guys make out."

"Let's just say that when it comes to mating, we return to our roots. And I must say there is some logic to it. Adrenaline's a potent arouser." He bumped her hips with his, leaving no question as to the potency of his arousal. "So, was it as good for you as it was for me?"

Eva was surprised to realize he wasn't the only one reacting to an adrenaline rush. "Strange, but it is pretty exhilarating. How about another 'kiss'?"

"The kiss I want to give you . . ." He studied her for a bit,
then shook his head. "Too much, too soon. Like discovery,
we'll get where we're going when you're ready to be there."
A lick to her chin was followed by the graze of his teeth. "But
you're a quick study and we'll get there soon enough."

Hesitantly, she asked, "Get where?"

"For now . . ." His lips on hers, she heard the snap of his
fingers. And then she heard voices all around, felt the support of his arms about her, and planking beneath her feet.

Urich lifted his lips and she realized they were standing on
a pier at Fisherman's Wharf. No one in the crowd seemed to
notice that they'd been joined by a kissing couple who had
materialized out of nowhere.

"Ahh," Urich breathed. "Just smell all the teeming humanity. Except—ugh. There's some bad company we don't
need around." A yell and a splash later, he sighed happily.
"That's that. His date won't get raped tonight."

"Urich, you have to quit messing with—"

"Would you rather me let something terrible happen instead of doing what I can to stop it?"

"Of course not, but—"

"But what?"

No ifs, ands or buts about it, he was impossible. Absolutely, marvelously impossible.

"I'm crazy about you, too," he murmured, offering his
arm. "Let's go have some fun."

Strolling along the wharf, Eva's only pleasure was in
Urich's elation over the jugglers and musicians performing
for what landed in their instrument cases. As for herself, it
wasn't exactly peachy being with a head-turning hunk. She
wasn't sure if she felt closer to strutting like a peacock or

running around like a chicken with its head cut off, knocking over each and every drooling female.

"Look!" he exclaimed, pointing to a mime. "He reminds me of a dream weaver."

"What's a dream weaver?"

"They're enchanting creatures. Nothing logical about them, but they create the most splendid comedies and tragedies. Their world is real but it's not, like spun imaginings on paper. By the way, I've read all your books—Stephen King, now there's a dream weaver if there ever was one—and I'd really like to get my hands on some more."

She should be beyond surprise about anything by now, yet she gaped at him. "I must have a thousand books in my library. When did you have the time to read them?"

"It seemed a lot safer than watching you sleep when I couldn't sleep myself the last two nights, wanting you." Although his hands were on her shoulders, she could feel a brush between her thighs, more like a warm palm than the cool breeze skating up her legs. "Actually, you have a thousand and twenty books, but about fifty are missing the last chapters. Why did you tear them out?"

"I didn't like the endings, so I warmed my toes with them in the fireplace while I rewrote them in my head. I like my endings happy. I like to think the dragon could actually sleep with the dove." She ran a fingertip over the shawl's firebreathing dragon. "You remind me of a dragon."

"And you remind me of a dove." From thin air, Urich plucked one. Eva gasped in delight and they were joined by several others who watched him set it free. Seemingly oblivious to their small audience, he said, "Make that more like a flock of doves." With a sweep of his arms, a flock of fluttering gray wings swooped through the gathering crowd and up into the air.

"Wow!" shouted a child. "How did you do that?"

While Urich took in the riveted spectators and greeted them with a bow, Eva frantically wondered how they were going to get out of this one.

"Ladies and gentlemen," he announced, "allow me to introduce myself: Urich, master magician of the universe. Welcome to my world of wonders." While Eva silently prayed he wouldn't do anything too spectacular, he proceeded to do just that. Blowing her a kiss, he breathed fire from his dragon lips. Touching his fingertips to the dancing flame, sparks ignited on each one. Flicked to the sky, a shower of fireworks rained over the crowd, which was going wild.

"More! More! More!" came the roar amid deafening applause.

Urich reached into his pocket, then presented an orchid to a small girl at the front. "There's more where that came from," he said, shoving both hands into his pockets. Pulling them inside out, he said, "Now where did they go?"

"Here!" came a shout. And then another, and another, until there were enough orchids to fill a hothouse waving at Urich on the pier.

Eva felt a little cheated since she didn't get one.

But then he reached down the front of his shirt, and with a flourish pulled out a huge bouquet.

"For my lady," he said, presenting it to her with a bow.

As she accepted his offering and thrilled at the title, *his* "lady," Urich whispered, "Time to make a little magic of our own—alone."

As he pulled her beside him, his voice carried over the mass cheer going up.

"And now, for my final act, my assistant and I will disappear before your very eyes. Your shawl, please?" Urich gestured to the shawl and it floated from her shoulders to his. Sweeping her into his arms, he said, "Now you see us. And now you—" He snapped his fingers.

"Don't," he finished, just as they landed with a plop on her bed. The flowers crushed between his chest and hers, Urich chortled with glee and thrust them to the floor. "They smell good, but not nearly as sweet as you."

Touching his lips in mid-descent, she said, "What you gave those people was a wonderful thing. But Urich, what about the florist who's going to find an empty store?"

Always, he thought, she was always concerned about such things. It struck him that while he found her sterling ethics one of her most admirable qualities, it could be irritating. Especially when his own ethics would surely be bending at the meeting he was due at soon. And especially when he was in need of her giving touch to get him through what lay ahead.

"A hundred or so stores is more like it and they won't miss a flower or two. And as for what I did, the pleasure was more mine than theirs." Remembering that ocean of smiles and shining eyes, he was humbled and honored to know his talents could give so much pleasure to others. "It made me realize there's a better use for my gifts than I've put them to in the position I was given to serve."

"And just what exactly is that position, Urich?"

"An uncomfortable one," he said evasively. Enough of this conversation; it was getting too close for comfort when closeness was exactly the comfort he needed. Nuzzling deep between her thighs, he murmured, "Yes, I'm most uncomfortable at the moment. With your legs cradling mine, your breasts softer than the feathers of a dove, you're making me so hard that I hurt. Feel me hurt," he gently commanded, pressing deep into the warm hollow that he ached to fill until they were sealed tighter than a vise.

Shunting the image and the sensation it provoked from his mind to hers, he heard Eva moan long and low in her throat as he licked it. The urge to mark her was too great and he tongued his way up to her lips before he demanded, pleaded, that she ask for The Kiss.

A safer kiss he gave, ravaging her mouth and funneling all his dark desires within it. And he took, took, took, all that bright glorious light of her soul that she shared without reserve. It made him greedy for more and he pawed roughly at her breasts. And what comfort it was that she didn't shrink from the animal who began to hump upon her in a frenzy, but met him in kind while scratching wildly at his back.

So caught up in the madness, he didn't realize where it was leading until she had wedged a hand between them. Tugging urgently at his zipper, she cried, "Help me. Take off your pants, get rid of my hose, *be inside me.*"

Urich suddenly went still. Eva had no idea what she was trying so desperately to unleash. And The Kiss had to come first, *had to*. Much as he was deserting the ways of his people, this was one code of honor he could not break. Powerful as his lust for her was, his respect for the mate he would take went deeper. As did his love.

They were enough to jolt him into action before it was too late. With a snarl, he flung himself off. Off her, off the bed. He had to get out. He was halfway there when she caught up. Jerking him around, she demanded, "Where do you think you're going?"

"Anywhere but in reach of you. Believe me, Eva, you don't want me to stay. If I do . . ." He touched her neck, then withdrew with a tortured groan. "I'll be back."

He made it as far as the door before he heard the stamp of a foot. "You just stop right there! Damn you, Urich, how dare you do this to me. Again! Every time you get me so hot that I'm scorched from the heat, you dump cold water all over us. And then you have the nerve to act like you're doing me some kind of favor."

"I am." The gaze he turned on her was ferocious in its hunger, all but snapping her up in a single bite.

But instead of warning her off, it seemed to incite her all the more. "I don't believe you, you—"

"Yes?" he challenged, crushing the doorknob in his fist.

She seemed to search for an epithet that was adequately scathing to describe what she thought of his "favor" of withholding his favors. Finding a deserving word, she hurled it at him: "You're a beast!"

Silence pulsed like the beat of his heart, a war drum that gave way to the sound of metal stripping metal.

"More than you know, Eva." He tossed the mangled knob to her feet, then swung wide the ungutted door. A flash of his teeth and he passed a hand over his loins as he again advised her, "More than you know."

12

"YOU'RE LATE."

"An unavoidable detainment." Urich offered no explanation to either Raven or Zar. He resented having to tear himself away from Eva. He'd waited until she slept, then stolen into her dreams to tell her it was love that had made him leave her, that he'd come too close to giving her The Kiss. A kiss that would bind them beyond human vows, allow them to share an intimacy beyond human capability.

"Your gaze is distant and strangely... soft." Zar frowned. "Where are your thoughts—since they're obviously not on this meeting?"

This meeting is a travesty of justice, Urich wanted to rail. Knowing such an accusation would stir their suspicions, he hardened his gaze on Zar.

"True, my mind isn't here. If you ventured among humans I'm sure you'd find your thoughts distracted, too."

"There is only one human we're concerned with," Raven interjected. "How goes your progress with her?"

"It's none—" *of your business!* "It's none too easy. She's a complicated creature, as all humans are. They're a mire of emotional contradictions, and quite convoluted in their reasoning. Highly interesting."

"Enough of 'they.' What of *she?*" Zar pressed.

His father's interest in Eva ground like nails against teeth. Urich silently gnashed his.

"She accepts me for what I am."

"Then she's ready to accept us and lend her assistance," was Zar's eager conclusion.

"No." A thousand times *no!* "She can accept me because I exhibit enough human qualities to put her at ease. The rest of you, however, lack the nature to give her a sense of comfort and connection."

"If this 'comfort and connection' is essential for her cooperation, then I'll do what I must to promote it." Zar's sigh was one of resignation. "I'll study this nature of humans and emulate the necessary behavior."

"An exercise in futility," Urich smugly advised him. "You don't have the skill."

"And what skill would that be?"

"The ability to feel."

Zar appeared puzzled; Raven fairly cringed. He knew of the lipstick and had obviously kept that to himself—along with his awareness of the attraction Urich had confessed to.

There had been whispered rumors that Raven had loved his mate, and that misfortune had been coupled with the tragedy of her loss. It had supposedly happened long before Urich was born, and although he'd never given the rumor credence, the flash of compassion in Raven's eyes gave him away.

The brief connection of their gazes relayed infinitely more than they'd ever spoken in a vastness of Earth years.

Raven lowered his eyes and began to pace the alloy floor. How cold it was, Urich thought, already missing the warmth of wood.

"It would seem we have a problem that defies a logical solution," Raven finally said.

"Nothing defies a logical solution," Zar pronounced with the absolute authority his son had once admired.

"Humans do." Urich said it with the authority he now prized above his father's. "If you don't believe me, why don't you pay a visit yourself? You just might find Earth as disarmingly delightful and deliciously decadent as I do."

"Considering how oddly this place and these beings have affected you, I don't want to risk a similar contamination."

"I see. You didn't mind Mylar risking it and raised only minor objections to my exposure, but consider yourself either too weak or too worthy to do the same."

"How dare you speak to me as if I were a coward!" In a few swift strides Zar came within touching distance but stopped short of jabbing a finger into the wayward son's chest. "You know why I can't place myself in jeopardy."

Indeed he did, but sympathy for Zar's position was beyond him. And he certainly wasn't about to deliver the apology his father was waiting for.

He glanced at Zar's clenched fist. Deducians were averse to touching and he took a perverse pleasure in goading Zar to contact him for one of the few times in their lives.

"You want to hit me, don't you? Go ahead. Do it and see what it feels like. Consider it an experience in human nature I'm offering in return for offending you. No need to worry that I'll strike back, since your safety is something I wouldn't dream of jeopardizing."

"Why, you—you—" Zar smacked his fist into his palm.

"Careful, you're beginning to sound almost human. You're even close to looking like one of those Trojans on a gaming field ready to tackle an opponent. Football, they call it. Most entertaining. Barbarically so."

Zar's anger gave way to an expression of incredulity. "You can't possibly approve of such things."

"But I do. It's fun. So is eating junk food, wearing jeans and sweatshirts, watching movies." *Holding hands, kissing soft lips, playing magician, giving Eva flowers . . .*

"I don't believe what I'm hearing! Listen to yourself, Urich. First you insult me, then you praise their heathen customs as if they were superior to our own. What has this place done to you?"

Before Urich could lash out with an incriminating answer, or a fist of his own—would it feel as satisfying as a hug?— Raven hurried toward them to intercede.

"Calm yourself, Zar. Urich was simply trying to help you gain a better understanding of Dr. Campbell's race. This is the sort of irrational behavior her kind displays, and since no amount of reasoning can explain it, he thought it easier to show than to tell." He glanced sharply at Urich. "Correct?"

"Thank you, Raven." He owed him more than his thanks. "This is what I'm dealing with there. Abysmal, isn't it?"

"Horrifying," concurred Zar. "No wonder Mylar met such a terrible fate. I thought it due to his empathic abilities, but given your own report, we could never adapt to this crude planet. We'll continue to search for another while going ahead with our initial plan."

Urich's narrow escape had led to an iron trap that slammed down on his heart. He wanted Eva by his side. He wanted the company of humans, one of the cigarettes he had inhaled, a newspaper and a La-Z-Boy recliner with Eva on his lap.

It would defy their comprehension; he didn't understand it himself, but still he *felt* these yearning desires.

Choosing his words with far more care than he had his previous ones, Urich chanced saying, "Crude as human nature is, there are many wonderful things about it, as well. For all that's unpleasant, a wealth of goodness prevails. My choice of example was negative and I should have selected better."

"Such as?" Zar looked dubious.

"When humans argue, they make amends in various and charming ways. Between men it usually involves a handshake. It's often used for greetings and partings, too. Here,

I'll show you." He made a long reach and clasped his father's stiff hand, shaking it briefly.

Zar discreetly wiped his palm on his thigh.

"Humans like to touch," Urich advised him. "You might even come to enjoy it yourself if you tried it more often."

"I doubt that—at least when it comes to males. But what of women?" His expression said he wouldn't find that contact nearly so distasteful. "How do they express amends?"

Urich knew he'd cut his tongue out before saying they liked to kiss and make up. "Why don't you come visit and find out yourself? An afternoon in the company of humans—" *Many humans... many, many women. Exactly!* "You'll be safe. In fact, you might be pleasantly surprised at how enjoyable their habitat can be. You could try their food, see them play on a field of grass and perhaps even dance with one of their females. Dancing, very quaint. And I can't even describe how flattering it is to be looked at by these Earth women. They call us 'hunks.' Our features are highly attractive to them."

Zar stepped back as if he might contract whatever illness was affecting Urich's reason.

"Raven, you go. If you return speaking a similar gibberish, we'll retrieve Urich and take the female with him. She'll surely adjust better to us than we possibly could to her species." That said, he left.

Once alone, Raven whirled on Urich. "I should have let you hang yourself!"

"But you didn't. And Raven, we both know why."

"Don't remind me. I've spent most of my existence trying to forget the very thing you're battling now." He shut his eyes as if battling his own reason's loss all over again. "Don't let it win, Urich. For your sake, for all our sakes, don't let it win."

"Too late, I'm...a goner—as they say on Earth. As for why you'd want to forget what was surely the most marvelous occurrence in your life, it makes no more sense to me than propagating a race that can contribute nothing but logic to a universe that could learn more from humanity than it ever could from us."

Raven paled. "It seems you're dangerously close to becoming more human than not."

"I can only hope so."

"This goes from worse to worse to worse." Wearily sinking into a rigid chair, Raven slumped forward.

Urich laid a hand on Raven's shoulder, startling him. "I wanted to console you," he explained. "It's one of the good things I've experienced. When you come—say, in two Earth weeks—I'll share some of these pleasures with you. I think you'll have fun."

"And if I do, you'll want me to keep my silence about that from Zar, along with the rest." He scowled. "It will all come to light eventually. And when it does, you can claim temporary insanity, while I'll have no excuse for being a co-conspirator in abetting this madness. Not that I care to keep what life I have left, but my honor will be tarnished and that's worse than death."

"You show a greater honor now and for that I'm eternally grateful. No one will know about this but us," he assured. "As for claiming insanity, I couldn't dishonor the truth of my emotions any more than I could give Eva over into Zar's hands."

"His impatience allows you little time to find a solution— if one exists." Then, as if unable to resist heaping some misery on the source of his own, he said bluntly, "You have only yourself to blame for the entire situation. It was *you* who convinced the Tribunal that only Dr. Campbell would do."

"She was the logical choice—at the time," he defended.

"And now?"

"Eva's still the best." He felt Raven shudder at his lethal whisper: "But Raven, she's *mine*."

FOR A LONG TIME Urich gazed at her, so peaceful and trusting in sleep's repose. He longed to claim that peace, some of that sense of trust, for himself.

When he told Eva, as inevitably he must, of his leading role in her willing capture, her trust in him would have every reason to waver.

And just how far could he trust Raven?

Although Raven sympathized, his reluctant assistance was as borrowed as the time running out with each tick of the clock.

Time. How swiftly he was changing. His thoughts and emotions were in metamorphosis, working an odd effect on his abilities.

He hadn't been able to read Zar's mind or influence his decision to visit Earth—an idea more desperate than plausible. It seemed when he needed his talents the most, they had deserted him. The only logical explanation was that he couldn't control another when his own mind was in chaos.

Eva was a haven, one he sought as he lay beside her and gently turned her onto her back. Beneath the thin white gown her breasts sloped gracefully, beckoning him to tug loose the pink satin ribbon and expose the loveliness of her flesh.

"Urich?" she murmured groggily.

"Here, Eva." For now—and if the gods were merciful, for always.

"I was dreaming of you. Something about a kiss." She opened her arms to him. "Kiss me? A kiss to make up."

"Then you're not mad at me anymore?"

"All I'm mad about is you."

Her lips, her embrace, the whole of her was like holding heaven in his arms while all around them was the nightmare he had spun better than a Dreamweaver from hell.

I need you, Eva. God, how I need you. Hold me, just hold me and give me some of your peace.

"Anything I have is yours," she whispered, urging him to her breast. "Nurse from me and find some peace there."

Urich blessed her for those powers she had returned to him. She cleansed his mind and brought pure vision to his heart. The vision of her breast, where her own heart beat, was beyond resistance.

His lips descended and he filled his mouth with her, suckled like a hungry babe drinking in a sweet, deep peace.

13

WHAT TO DO WITH himself until Eva returned home from work? Another video didn't hold much appeal after watching ten on fast-forward in less than an hour. A book? He supposed he could scan what little remained in the local library that he'd yet to read. Or, he could make a lunch of Milky Way bars—

"Damn," he muttered, remembering he'd finished off the box last night.

With a sigh of frustration, Urich wondered if what he was feeling was boredom. It would be the first time he'd experienced it in the two weeks he had lived with Eva.

She made even little things seem like fun. The time they spent together was always special, whether exploring the city she didn't want him to venture about without her, or conferring on that rudimentary project of hers that she wanted to compensate him for.

He didn't want her money for something he found so simple yet so pleasurable in working toward a mutual goal. They'd argued about the pay issue and even that had been exciting—their logical debate giving way to an emotional clash, then kissing to make up once they'd reached a compromise: He would accept just enough to take her out and buy a few necessities.

So far that included sodas and candy bars, video rentals and little presents for Eva when they went shopping. A dozen pairs of stockings after she'd ranted over a run in her new hose. Ten tubes of the lipstick she had raved over because it stayed put for hours and didn't kiss off on him or a glass.

Urich clinked the ice cubes in his empty glass. A six-pack of colas downed since she'd left for work; he'd hit his sugar-high limit. A beer was tempting but he knew better than to take so much as a sip.

One sip and he'd surely go over the edge he was skating on. To look at her, just to think of her was to be seized with the compulsion to mark her. *Was she ready?*

It was the question he asked himself each night that ended with the passionate kisses he cooled—only for Eva to be so frustrated that she sent him out the bedroom door he'd yet to fix. A reminder. He'd left it to impress upon her just what she'd be dealing with if they crossed the line from kissing companions to what they both ached to be.

Lovers, of course. The problem was, he dared not make love to her like a man, knowing it would trigger the trans-formation. And once transformed, if she had the courage to witness that, then she'd have to ask for The Kiss.

The kiss of the beast. *That's* what she had to be ready for. While it would put an end to their mutually miserable yearn-ing to mate, it would be the beginning of a bond that only death could sever.

Enraptured as she was with him, was she prepared for such a significant commitment? For as long as it lasted, anyway? To give Eva his mark was beyond taboo, and while it would protect her for as long as he lived, his days would be num-bered if the Tribunal discovered his crime of passion.

As they would unless he could come up with a solution— and he was no closer to a workable one than he had been the last time he'd seen Raven.

Two days to go before Raven's scheduled visit. Eva was looking forward to meeting this "colleague" of his who had relayed a wish to join them for reasons of curiosity.

Deciding to put the afternoon to good use, Urich took to the streets that Eva didn't want him wandering by himself. He wouldn't get into one of those jams she worried about him being stuck in without her there to play mediator. And he'd make sure he was back before she returned from work.

He had some work to see to himself. A sweet treat for Raven wasn't a bad idea.

Especially if she was desirable enough for him to want to take more than a nibbling bite of his own.

"JEEZ, EVA, three o'clock and you're out of here? The party's just getting started. Don't tell me you've got a hot date."

"You could sound a little less amazed by the possibility, Ethan."

With an edge of distress he said, "So that is the rush, after all."

More like six phone calls in two hours with no answer from Urich, was the rush. But Ethan's unguarded expression stopped her flight out the door.

He looked crushed.

Eva was stunned. After five years of working more closely with Ethan than she'd ever snuggled in bed with John, she realized he had a thing for her. All his worrying about her safety, the cajoling to get together after work, had been personal.

How she'd missed something so obvious, Eva didn't know. Then again, a world of self-truths had been staring her in the face she hadn't seen them until she'd fallen into Urich's looking-glass gaze.

Her own softened on Ethan. "Actually, that's not why I'm leaving early." He looked hopeful.

Too hopeful. Tempering his expectations, she said, "Four experiments in as many days and I'm ready to celebrate with a hot bath and a good book."

"Wouldn't you rather celebrate together? I mean, the holodeck's about as perfected as it can get and our funders are thrilled, raving about our success."

Success? Her brainchild was a crude invention compared to Urich's technology. Yet he found her work enchanting, delighted in giving her "hints" to refine their project, and expressed admiration for her mental acuity after she'd fried her mind to come up with what was as easy as two-plus-two to him.

Success? The way she figured it, having Urich in her life was the kind of personal fortune that put professional achievement in its proper perspective.

"You're right, Ethan. As hard and long as we've worked together, we should celebrate together—another time. Sorry to be a party pooper, but I'm beat." Against her better judgment, she kissed his cheek.

Ethan touched it as he watched her race away. Just as well, since he could feel himself blushing. Not that he was a virgin or something, but this was Eva. He was nuts about her; had been for years.

Come her divorce, he'd been overjoyed. But it hadn't changed anything. She never let him get closer than the picture he'd ripped from a *VR World* magazine—the two of them huddled together over a computer. He kept it beside his bed.

Shutting the door to her office, he went to her desk. He'd picked the lock several times in search of a tube of her lipstick or a brush holding a few strands of her hair. Testing the drawer, it slid open. Wherever she was in such a hurry to get to, her haste had worked to his advantage.

Fingering her calculator, he imagined them crunching math formulas together. *Mmm.* Late into the night. *Oh, yes.* He'd ease behind her and rub her shoulders, massage her neck, slowly work his way down . . .

Whew. Better put that calculator back and go take a cold shower. But first, he'd play with her brush. The handle was wedged under a book. Curious as to what she was reading, he pulled out a textbook. On telekinesis?

Flipping through, a folded page of graph paper fell out. Some of her secret calculations? A love letter?

Unfolding it, his brow furrowed as he read, "Mind over matter," in big scrawled letters. But at the bottom she'd doodled hearts around the word, "Urich."

Putting everything back as he'd found it, Ethan had the unsettling hunch that he'd stumbled on something a lot more intimate than a love letter or a tube of lipstick.

WHERE WAS URICH? He'd promised not to wander the city alone until she was certain he could cope on his own. Trying to calm herself, Eva reasoned that he was somewhere within walking distance since he'd promised not to do any zapping, either. Much as she worried about any sticky situations he might encounter here, if he got into trouble on the globe's other side, there was no way she could help bail him out.

Leaving the house, she went in search. No sign of him strolling the streets. And his cravings for soda and chips and candy bars hadn't sent him to the grocery store for a junk-food fix. Maybe he was checking out the video stands. His appetite for musicals and Westerns was right up there with greasy popcorn.

"Sorry, he hasn't been here." The clerk who'd waited on them several times before sighed wistfully.

Eva knew she was sorry, all right. The girl fawned over Urich every time they came in. So did the elderly librarian, who gushed over his apparent love of books.

No matter the age, women couldn't take their eyes off him. It was to a point that Eva wanted to put a bag over his head in public so she wouldn't have to deal with her private distress.

But she couldn't do that anymore than she could keep him locked in the house while she went to work.

All she could do was trust him. Trust him not to break her heart. Trust he could take care of himself without her guiding presence.

He wouldn't need her to guide him much longer.

She didn't want to think about that. And she most certainly didn't want to think about what would happen to them once Urich had gotten all that he'd come for.

Passing an outdoor café, Eva hit the brakes.

Her stomach twisted. She was queasy, dizzy. She couldn't breathe. A horn honked behind her and Eva forced her foot onto the accelerator.

By some miracle she made it home. She hadn't seen the stop signs or traffic negotiated. All she'd been able to see, continued to see, was Urich. Urich sitting at a table, his attention riveted on another woman.

A very pretty woman who had laughed and touched his hand.

ONE GLIMPSE OF EVA'S CAR in the driveway and Urich knew he'd been caught.

Testing his acquired skills, he considered a variety of human responses: He could take the defensive and bluster about her going to work while he twiddled his thumbs and she had no right to be mad when he had every right to spend his hours alone as he pleased.

Too . . . juvenile and aggressive.

Should he just simply apologize for what he wasn't at all sorry for? That one he dismissed even faster than the first. Besides being dishonest, it implied his need for her permission, as though he were a child and not a man who could make his own decisions.

Yes, it was time Eva accepted his ability to interact with others and not worry about his social skills. Why, they were becoming impeccable. He hadn't taken his eyes off Justine from the moment she'd asked to share his table. Eva would be proud that he'd mastered that lesson—one that had led to his winning Justine's eager acceptance for a date with Raven. Not only did she profess a weakness for older men, she couldn't wait to meet him since Urich had assured her that Raven was just as "yummy" and charming as she thought he was.

Charm. That was it! He'd sweet-talk his way into her arms and they'd get this settled, easy as pie.

"Eva? Oh, honey, I'm ho-ome!" Chuckling at the domestic greeting, savoring the endearment, he bounded up the stairs that led to a bedroom filled with feminine smells and trinkets, frivolous furniture and enticing attire.

Oh, but he loved it, loved it all. But more than anything, he loved Eva. Once Raven met her, he would understand why. As for himself, he couldn't wait to kiss her as senseless as she'd rendered him. *Tonight.* Tonight could be the night that ended with more than human kisses.

His teeth were still tingling from the thought when he came to her knobless door. Shut. Surely she wasn't still upset about his departure last night. Or his string of profanities when she broke his ravenous kiss to make up this morning. After all, he had promised to curb his foul language.

Whatever the reason for her shutting him out, he didn't like it. Clamping down the urge to smack open the door and demand immediate possession of her mouth, her breasts— sweet heavens above, her breasts. One look, one taste of a woman's breast and there wasn't a Deducian male in existence who'd have a stitch of logic left.

What little logic he had remaining advised him to block out the emotions he lacked mastery of and politely knock.

No answer.

But he could hear her moving about.

He knocked again. Still no answer. Urich booted open the door.

She was riffling through her closet. He wanted to know why she hadn't asked him in, but there was a stiffness in the back she kept turned to him that advised him to proceed with more caution than charm. A warm greeting seemed wise.

"I missed you today, Eva."

Ignoring him, she pulled out a little black dress. Then went to her chest of drawers. There, she deliberated over the variety of panties and bras and hosiery, which she dangled within his vision, one by one, before settling on the most arousing of the combination.

He was aroused from simply watching.

"You're teasing me, aren't you?" he asked, moving behind her and catching at the lacy panties she held.

She yanked them away and the gaze she turned on him could have chipped ice. "If I wanted to tease you, I'd do this." She put a palm to his crotch and squeezed.

A bit too hard. He winced and she let go.

"If you must know, I'm going out. Now get out so I can change." She was halfway to the door he was certain she meant to slam behind him when he swung her around to face him.

"If that's what you're wearing to go out, you're not leaving without me."

"Sorry, Urich, but you're not invited."

She was meeting a man; her selected items left no question about it. An awful sensation gripped him, clawing and tearing at his heart, blinding him with jealous rage.

"Who is he?" Gritting out the words took enormous control. He wanted to shake her, go hunt down the man and rip out his throat. "Tell me!" he demanded.

"I don't have to tell you anything." She shoved at his chest and he tightened his grip. "Damn you, let go."

Once he'd dropped her onto the bed, he did. "There."

When she started to scoot off, he shoved her back. Looming over her, he warned, "Move again and I'll be on you. The beast within is demanding his due and the only thing that's stopping him is a fragment of reason. I suggest you nourish it by explaining just what the hell is going on."

"Why don't you read my mind and tell me? No need to knock, come right on in."

His own mind was too crowded to get into hers, and so he said flatly, "No."

"Then I guess you'll just have to draw your own logical conclusions."

She looked away as if she couldn't stand the sight of him. Was she deliberately trying to drive him mad with the riddle of her behavior? If so, Eva was dangerously close to succeeding. So many feelings were welling inside him, he could barely think past the instinct to pounce, proclaim his possession of a mate who would bare her throat in submission.

A snarl escaped him, trembling the charged air.

The hair on her nape prickled. Eva glanced warily at Urich. His gaze was on her neck and his upper lip curled above those gleaming, canine incisors.

He had warned her and she had provoked him, too hurt to be honest and too angry to take heed. The hurt wasn't gone and neither was the anger, but those teeth of his had a way of putting both into perspective.

"Maybe we should talk, Urich."

His answer was another snarl, his hands moving to his shirt, a savage yank that stripped buttons from thread. With his gaze fixing her there, she felt like a bird held in thrall by a predator, a doe blinded by glass-green lights.

She couldn't move, but at least her vocal chords still worked, just barely, allowing her to stutter, "I—I saw you with a—another woman."

"For Raven," he growled, his hands going to his pants.

Relief washed over her while the tide of alarm rose.

Eva began talking. Fast. "I'm sorry, really sorry for thinking you were sneaking around with another woman but after John I don't trust men or aliens or anything male and it's a problem I've got that I thought I was past but I'm apparently still dealing with. I'll learn from my mistake and trust you next time, okay?"

She heard the whisper of his belt sliding from denim, the metal buckle hitting the floor.

"N-now that we've got that settled, why don't we talk about this woman you found for Raven? Or—or we could talk some more about his visit." The pound of a war drum seemed to echo from wall to wall, matching the thrumming of her heart. "Hey, I've got an idea! Want to see if we can get tickets to next Sunday's game? My treat, even at scalpers' prices."

She heard the hiss of his zipper. She would have looked if she could. But even her peripheral vision was locked on his dilated pupils—two black full moons, sucking her in.

In a tremulous whisper she said, "I'm suddenly starved. Let's go out to eat. What're you hungry for?"

Teeth bared, he licked them. *"You."*

14

HE COULD SEE, FEEL her shaking, shaking from head to toe. His inner smile was grim. For all the lessons that Eva had taught him, Urich deemed her in need of one herself.

She had awakened the beast within and he was restless. But fortunately for Eva, her confession had wooed reason and the leash still held. Barely. Had she continued with her little tortures, he would have snapped. It was imperative that she realized the price attached to inflicting such womanly wiles upon him.

Next time, she might not be so lucky.

"The wolf is near," he told her as closer he approached. "You taunted him to come and he's hungry for more than a bite."

Urich snapped his teeth and he could hear her tight swallow. "Call to the lioness, Eva. You'll need her to fight the beast you bring out in me. But he'll win and you'll need her even more to survive his possessing."

"I belong to myself," she said with admirable bravado.

He leaned over her and slid a palm up her dress. Cupping her as she had him, he squeezed. But his squeezing was a seductive grip and release, grip and release. Feeling her in his hand, so warm and moist, hearing her moan, he knew his never-ending need to possess her had to be appeased.

But he couldn't force that ultimate decision. He could only coax her closer to the line he had drawn and they were destined to cross. Wooing her body with a gentle persuasion, he carefully chose the words that would lead to the end of their beginning and begin the journey to their ultimate end.

"Yes, Eva, you do belong to yourself—just like we belong together. Never doubt it. But most of all, never doubt your power over my body, even my soul. You did and that's why you doubted me. To be all that we can be, you have to tell me your true feelings instead of letting them fester and wedge us apart. Promise you won't do that again."

"Promise," she said, pulling him down beside her and moving into the grip of his hand.

His free hand reached for hers. "Yours is the only hand I've ever held. Your breasts the only breasts I've ever touched. And your lips the only ones I've ever kissed. I don't need any others, Eva, and never would I want them. It's the nature of the beast. But he demands an equal fidelity from his mate for as long as he lives, and should you *ever* wander . . . the penalty's severe. The instinct for absolute possession is stronger in me than any amount of humanity I could ever acquire. It's a binding decision I'm after and one for you to think hard about."

Think? How was she supposed to think with his pants open just far enough to show he had no underwear on, luxurious soft hair playing in counterpoint to the hard ridge of his pubis rubbing against her thigh.

"Is—is this a 'till death do us part and you're dead if you ever cheat on me' pop of the question?"

His gaze was as steely as the concealed arousal he pressed hard against her leg. "Human vows aren't as binding as those I'd have you take with me. Never to be parted once paired. Cleave to another and I'll unman him while you watch."

"That's brutal!"

"A brutally fit punishment for an even crueler crime against your mate. We don't take infidelity lightly—which is why it simply doesn't happen with my kind. The same goes for treason. The penalty for *that* is death."

"But you said your people weren't violent."

"They aren't. They're much too civilized to do any killing of another. But honor can demand that one kill himself. Honor, Eva, is as entrenched in me as fidelity."

There was a flash of silver in his eyes. She saw it as she had the first time she'd stepped through the looking glass of his gaze.

"Who died besides your mother, Urich?"

"Many have died, few remain."

Searching his eyes she saw once more a heartache to rival her own.

"You've loved someone and lost them, haven't you?"

Slowly, he shook his head. "Only you, Eva. Only you."

"But you haven't lost me."

"I pray I never do." And then he murmured, "The future can, and does, change."

Urich had seen the future and his cryptic remark left her floundering, clutching at him with fear of what it was that he had seen. She opened her mouth to demand he tell her but his palm came down, muffling her frantic words.

"Have you forgotten all that you've learned? Get rid of your fear, Eva. It's a poison that weakens and erodes your inner power, your strength. You'll need both and so will I to overcome the obstacles we have ahead."

He removed his hand and she struggled to tamp down her fear and find the courage to hear whatever he would tell her.

"And just what are these obstacles?"

"The Tribunal stands between us. They'll want me back, along with the use of my powers, to serve as Raven's next-in-command. Raven's sympathetic, and begrudging of it, but he can be trusted for now. I'm hoping the woman I found for him will secure his interest in helping me. He's very powerful, second only to my—our ruler."

His gaze seared into her and she saw the shade of his passion, a full moon eclipsed by a consuming sun.

"You're mine, Eva. *Mine.* And I'll die before ever giving you up." Suddenly, he delved beneath her hose and with a single fingertip, touched her cleft.

Eva nearly came off the bed. A thousand tiny vibrators were centered on that small pinnacle of flesh. Her immediate climax was jolting, the sensation so intense that she screamed. Screamed and screamed until she pleaded for him to stop before he killed her with ecstasy.

Removing his hand, he lay flush atop her. Long ebony hair streaming over her face, he swept it away with a toss of his head, like an animal shaking its mane.

And like an animal just finished with a fresh feast, he licked his fingertip, then smacked his lips—unsparingly sensual lips that curved into a cunning smile.

"I'd never stray. And neither would you. Not even before our inevitable mating." Loftily he raised an eyebrow. "Now, where were you going that I wasn't invited, and with whom were you planning to meet?"

The phone rang. *Oh, no, oh, no, not now.*

"I'll get it." Urich's hand shot out, intercepting hers. "Hello?" he politely answered, holding the earpiece close enough for her to listen in.

"Sorry, I must have the wrong number. This isn't . . ."

While he recited her number, Eva whispered, "Give me that. It's Ethan."

"Yes, I know," Urich whispered back. Then to Ethan he replied, "You must be calling for Eva."

"Well . . . yeah." *And who the hell are you?*

Why, the stinker! Urich wasn't content with the phone, he was telegraphing Ethan's private thoughts to her.

"I'm Urich. And you're Ethan, right? Eva's assistant."

Oh, so you're Urich. Move over, bud, no more Mr. Nice Guy, I'm putting the move on her tonight.

How did he know Urich's name? Had Ethan been snooping in her desk? Urich confirmed that suspicion with a nod.

"I'm not her assistant. I'm her associate. And you?"

"Why don't you ask Eva? I'll put her on." His deadly look didn't mesh with his pleasant, "Nice talking to you. I look forward to meeting . . . soon?"

He gave her the phone with a gloating smile. Eva wasn't sure whom she wanted to smack the most—Urich for his sneaky revelations or Ethan for the snooping she couldn't confront him with. To hell with them both; she wasn't up to either.

Her shaky, "Hi, Ethan. Sorry I'm—*late!*" coincided with Urich's thrust between her legs.

"Sounds like you have company."

"Urich. He's—he's—" He was nipping at her palm. "He's a special friend." His frown said that wasn't good enough. "An old companion." Still not good enough. "A mentor?" So-so, implied his shrug. "Let's just say that our relationship's unique and Urich would like to meet you." Big nod. "He's from out of town. *Way* out of town."

"If you'd told me when you called, I would have made an extra reservation." *Not.* "As it is, they're really crowded and I'm waiting at the bar. Our table's supposed to be ready in about thirty minutes but I'll tell them to give it to someone else. We'll take what's available after you get here."

With no way out of the predicament she'd gotten herself into, Eva agreed and hung up with a groan.

Urich was looking a mite too superior for her liking as he said, "So it goes when one acts before considering the consequences of a decision made out of passion or spite." He leaped off the bed, braced his feet on the floor and gestured toward his open fly. Thick whorls of gleaming black hair enticed her for a closer inspection of its source. But when she reached to touch, he stepped back and slid up his zipper.

"Take off your pants," she demanded, going after him.

"Another time—when passion leads me to act on that decision before I fully consider the consequences of it."

"You're being coy," she accused.

"And you're curious." He laughed darkly. "As well you should be. Unfortunately, you'll have to wait. Ethan's waiting and you're late."

"But I don't want to go!"

"You're the one who called him," was his nose-rubbing reminder. "Here, let me help you along. The sooner you go, the sooner you'll be back. And *if* I'm feeling generous, then maybe I'll let you appease your curiosity. But I wouldn't count on it since 'generous' is the last thing I'm feeling."

"Damn you, Urich! You're baiting me and—" He cut her off with a wave of his hand. *Whoosh. Whoosh.* Eva gaped at the sexy outfit she'd selected to spite him earlier and from which her breasts now spilled out.

"The hair should go up and the makeup on to suit the rest." The rest was waterfall rhinestone earrings, a matching choker; stockings with black seams up the back, and the stiletto-high heels she'd bought on a whim but had lacked the nerve to wear.

"Stop this!" she yelled, stamping a decadent heel.

"Just the finishing touches and I'll be done." He ended with a flourish and gave her a little push toward the mirror. "What do you think?"

What she thought was that she looked like Kim Basinger turning tricks for more money than she got paid to act.

Eva glared at him. "The mole has to go."

He pinched her cheek. "I like it. So will Ethan."

"You're being mean."

"Yes," he agreed, patting her rear. "But at least I'm honest about it. If you'd been honest with me, all of this could have been avoided."

"I promised to talk to you the next time instead of jumping to conclusions, didn't I? What else do you want?"

He toyed with a strand of hair cascading from her temple. A soft kiss came unexpectedly before he said with a quiet passion, "I want to make love to you like a man. I want to hump you like the animal I can be. I want you to think of me, of us, every second you're with him. And I want you to know that I trust you implicitly—even dressed like this."

"Of course, you can trust me. But Ethan . . . he'll get the wrong idea and he's got enough wrong ideas already."

"But I want to taunt him. He'll have to look at what he wants but can't have. I won't be able to look but I'll know he's looking at what I will have. A fair exchange of mutual misery, don't you think?"

Eva cupped his cheek and he pressed his lips into her palm. "Misery does like company, Urich. But that doesn't make it right. This isn't right."

Scowling, he appeared to consider what she had said. And finally, he sighed. "Life isn't always fair."

"No. It's like that waitress you helped out, who you said was a really good person but life hadn't been so good to her. You can't change the life of everyone who's gotten a raw deal, because we all get raw deals along the way. The color of life isn't black-and-white, Urich. It's one big shade of gray and we make it the best we can. And the best any of us can do is simply try to do the right thing."

"You make it sound so simple."

"It's not simple at all. If it was, I wouldn't be dreading a dinner I've got no one but myself to blame for, Ethan wouldn't be picking my lock and nursing false hope for something that's not going to happen, and you wouldn't be wanting your pound of flesh for being wronged." She pecked his cheek, then glanced at her watch. "I really hate it, but I have to go. If it'll make you feel better, I'll wear this so you can take some satisfaction in getting your just deserts."

She picked up the sequined purse and black silk shawl that had appeared on her dresser and made her way to the door.

"Eva."

"Yes?" She turned and he took her in from head to toe with a lustful yearning, heating and tantalizing her in places unseen.

"You look ravishing." He touched his chest where his heart beat. Then, sweeping the air, he bowed to her.

"Thank you, Urich." Eva laid her palm over her breast, her own heart beating for him, only for him. The power suit she now wore was just what she needed to set Ethan straight with the confidence she felt in herself. And in Urich. Beaming at him, she said, "You did the right thing. You should feel proud of yourself."

"I do. But even more, I feel...horny." With a wicked grin, he flicked his fly. "Hurry home, honey."

15

URICH GLOWERED at the television screen, impatient for Eva to get home.

He trusted her. Ethan, he did not.

Was she on her way? Or was Ethan putting the move on—as intended—while Eva rebuked his advances?

She wouldn't like him checking up on her, but there was no reason she had to know. He'd simply do a little astral projecting and assure himself of her safety.

Closing his eyes, Urich scanned the city for some sign of Eva. He spied her in a dimly lit parking lot. Ethan was reaching for her and she was shaking her head, grasping at the car door.

Honing in on their conversation, he heard Eva say, "Look, Ethan, we've worked together for years and it's been great. Let's not make things weird at work with more than a handshake good-night."

"I need more than a handshake, for once, Eva. Yeah, I admit it, I have gone through your desk. But only because it was as close as I could get to you."

"You're getting a little too close for comfort."

Ethan gripped her shoulders, pinned her against the car. "I say we're not close enough. What are you afraid of? That if I kiss you, you just might decide that you like it enough to do some experimenting together that doesn't have a damn thing to do with work?"

"I'm saying good-night now, Ethan. When I see you at work on Monday, we'll pretend we didn't have this conversation."

"I'm through pretending, Eva." When she tried to break free, he gripped her tighter. "Kiss me." His mouth going to the cheek she turned, he demanded, "Damn it, kiss me!"

A snap later, Urich tapped Ethan's shoulder.

"Huh?" Ethan turned his head, glared up at him. "I don't know who you are, but this is between me and the lady."

"Let her go."

"I'm not going to hurt her if that's what you're worried about. We've just got something to settle and you're not needed." Ethan turned back to Eva, who looked both gratefully and furiously at Urich.

He tapped again—hard enough to leave tiny bruises on the shoulders that bunched in angry reflex.

"I said, let her go. If you don't, I'll hurt you."

"He means it, Ethan." Eva glanced sharply at Urich, warning him off. Before she could introduce them or make excuses for his intrusion or diffuse the brewing fight—all of which Urich perceived she was about to do—Ethan whirled around.

He did some hard tapping himself at the massive chest he came shoulder-level to. "I don't know who you think you are, but I've had it with you. The lady's with me, understand?"

"What I understand is that she doesn't want you and if you value your body in one piece, then you'll say good-night like she asked." He gritted out his final warning for Ethan to leave, only Eva's presence staying him from launching the attack Ethan courted with a raised fist.

"No one's saying good-night but you!"

Urich gripped his fist and squeezed. "No one dares lay a hand on my—*oof!*" The punch to his stomach knocked the reason out of him and kicked in his instincts full throttle.

Seizing Ethan, Urich raised him over his head with a primal snarl.

"Help!" Ethan yelped. "Help!"

"Urich! Urich, put him down!" Eva cried while Ethan flailed like a speared fish in the hands held high in the air, poised to smash him to the pavement.

Eva's pleas cut through Urich's blinding rage and he grappled for the control he'd lost until Ethan's shouts of "Help!" mingled with a siren's scream.

"Oh, shit, oh, shit, not the police," Eva moaned as Ethan gasped, "The police, thank God, the police . . ."

Urich quickly returned Ethan to his feet—which buckled, his knees hitting ground—then said, "I'm sorry, Eva."

"Not half as sorry as you're gonna be once we're alone. Now zap yourself out of here. I'll handle the mess."

"It's my mess, not yours. I'm staying."

The slam of two car doors saved him an argument.

"What's going on here?" an officer demanded, partner in tow. "We got a call from someone who said there was a fight that was getting ugly."

"Man, am I glad to see you. He—he—"

"He was just trying to protect me, officer." Eva's quick defense won Ethan's dropped jaw and Urich's thin smile.

"Sounds like we need to have a little talk about this. On your feet, sir."

"But I . . . I . . . He . . . he . . ."

"It was a misunderstanding," Urich interjected as the officer helped Ethan to his feet. "I thought she was in danger and stepped in. But as it turned out he meant her no harm and my getting involved was a mistake."

"Ma'am? Is this true?"

"Yes, yes, it is. Everything's fine." She turned a pleading gaze on Ethan who was leaning against her car for support. "Right, Ethan?"

He darted a glance at the officer whose protection had turned in the favor of the monster he'd needed protection from. "Uh . . . right. There's no problem here."

"In that case, we'll leave and let the three of you do the same. But we'd better not get another call."

"You won't," Urich assured them and offered his hand to Ethan, who hesitated before chancing the grip. Satisfied, the police left the three of them alone.

Hands on her hips, Eva seethed, "Both of you should be ashamed of yourselves, making a scene like that!"

"Me? What'd I do besides try to kiss you before this—this freak nearly gave me a heart attack before he could splatter my guts on the ground?"

"The next time you try to kiss her, I will."

"What gives you the right to tell me that? And just what the hell are you, anyway? King Kong on steroids?"

"Eva is my woman and I protect what is mine. As for what I am—"

"That's enough out of both of you! Ethan, go home. Urich, go lift some weights if you want to let off some steam. As for me, I'm so steamed that I'm smokin'."

Ethan looked from one to the other. "Your woman? Does this mean that you two are, uh, like engaged or something?"

"Something and more," Urich confirmed. Eva didn't dispute him, but she looked mightily tempted to.

"Why didn't you tell me, Eva? You could have saved all of us a really nasty scene."

"That's a good question, Eva. Why didn't you tell him about us?"

Lips pinched, she glared at the two men who were waiting for an answer. It came to Urich that they'd put her in Ethan's earlier position, when he'd turned from victim to suspect. Suppressing a smile that would get him into more trouble than he already was, he offered, "Oh, of course. You wanted your family to be the first to know."

"Right," she said tightly. "Consider yourself honored, Ethan. You got the news before I had a chance to absorb it myself."

Although he surely considered the honor dubious, Ethan said quietly, "Congratulations."

"You're very gracious," Urich noted. "I'm impressed." Which he was. Even from Ethan, he was learning.

"And I'm envious as hell—but I know when I'm beat." Ethan breathed out a "Whew" as he sized up the winner. "So, you're a body builder. How much can you press?"

"I could go for a world record." He flexed an arm.

"I guess." Ethan eyed his biceps with even more envy than he'd expressed over Eva. "Wow, you snagged yourself a real Charles Atlas. He was my idol growing up. My dad gave me all those old books he'd ordered when he was a kid but—"

"I don't believe this." Eva rolled her eyes.

"Belief is the key," Urich explained. "You have to train your mind to achieve what you really want. Mind over matter."

"So that's— Never mind." Then to Eva, he said, "I pushed my luck and I'm really sorry about that. Guess getting those braces off went to my head. No hard feelings?"

"Of course not." Her shoulders stiffened as Urich put a possessive arm around them.

"Great. Maybe we can get together another time—make it a foursome—and Urich can give me some pointers Charles Atlas didn't cover." He laughed awkwardly.

"I'd like that," Urich told him, admiring Ethan's strained attempt at humor. "I hope you'll accept my apology for what I did. It was inexcusable."

"No sweat." This time Ethan didn't hesitate to shake the hand Urich proffered. "Later, Eva."

He was nearing his own car when she threw a quelling glance at Urich and broke away, caught Ethan's arm. She spoke quietly to him and although Urich wanted to listen, he did not. And when she kissed Ethan's cheek, he made himself watch, endured the flash of jealousy, and knew a small triumph in simply waiting as she gave Ethan an affectionate hug.

It was certainly more than she gave him upon returning. "Get in," she snapped.

Urich allowed her to drive several miles before breaking the terse silence. "Eva, I'm—"

"Don't talk to me, because anything I say back won't be nice." She slapped his hand away.

Her rejection stung. She wouldn't let him apologize, although Ethan, who'd been not only rejected but nearly mauled, had shown admirable grace in his acceptance. *Women.* Why did they say nothing was wrong when something was? Why, when they said something was wrong, did they lash out with silence and refuse to talk about it?

"Really, Eva, I don't under—"

"I said, don't talk to me."

He nursed his hurt and a growing indignation while she fumed in silence. By the time she killed the engine and marched into the house several paces ahead of him, the composure he had maintained was at an end.

Urich slammed shut the front door she'd left open. Eva stopped in her tracks, and slowly turned. Between gritted teeth, she punctuated each word. "This. Is. My. House. These. Are. My. Doors. Break another one and—"

"And you'll do what?" he challenged. "Spank me? Send me to my room? You're treating me like a child and I resent it."

"Then quit acting like one." She gave him her back. "Good night, Urich."

"Where do you think you're going?" His feet cut an aggressive path to the stairs before she could take to them.

"To my room. Alone."

"No, you're not. We're going to talk about why you're mad because I protected what was mine. And once you apologize to me for your rude rejection of my apology, then we'll kiss and make up. In bed. Together."

"I have no intentions of making up tonight and hell can freeze over before I apologize after you had the nerve to act like I'm your chattel! Well, I'm *not*. Do you hear me? I am not some kind of possession you can claim as yours, and nearly kill somebody over for something as minor as a kiss."

"You *are* mine. Mine to protect—with more care than I did earlier—and to kiss whenever I want. I want to kiss you now, Eva. *Now*."

"Too bad. I don't want to kiss you. If you're lucky, I'll wake up feeling otherwise." She tried to pass him but he latched onto her arms.

"You'll feel otherwise once I kiss you."

"Damn it, Urich, you're behaving worse than Ethan."

"He doesn't have a right to that behavior. I do," he informed her, scooping her up and making haste up the stairs.

"Put me down!"

He did. Plop in the middle of the bed, which he stood beside with legs braced and arms folded. "We'll finish our discussion and then I'll have that kiss you're withholding."

Rather than praise his restraint—the logical discourse he offered when they both knew he could have anything he wanted from her with a single well-placed fingertip—she threw a pillow at him. Smack in the mouth.

"That's the closest you're getting to a kiss tonight." She pointed to the door. "Out!"

Out? He'd give her "out," all right. Out of his clothes, out of hers. Out with her frustration and his reasons for sustaining it. And then out with her binding answer to seal their shared fates.

Slowly, with absolute purpose, Urich unbuttoned his shirt. Eva closed her eyes but he knew she was peeking beneath her lashes.

"Open your eyes," he softly commanded.

"No. You'll try to control me if I do."

"I don't want to control you. All I want or need from you is acceptance. Acceptance of my flaws and the best I have to offer. My fidelity, my devotion, my love. And my body's expression of them—such as my body is. Now, open your eyes and see what I am."

Hesitantly, she did. He watched her watching him as he released the snap on his jeans, then drew down the zipper. Although he wanted to close his eyes against any revulsion in hers, he had to know, had to see her acceptance or rejection as he pushed the jeans to his thighs.

No farther did he go, prepared to restore himself at a single shudder. No shudder came, but she did gasp.

Her hand trembled as she reached to touch him. The touch she blessed him with expanded both his heart and the loins she marveled over with whispers of wonder.

"You see as others do not, Eva."

"What I see is . . . Urich, you're breathtaking."

"I'll take yours away as never before," he vowed as she stroked his sheath. "Come, Beauty, come love your Beast."

16

THE TOUCH OF MINK. A fur so luxurious and sensual and soft, she would have wrapped her body in it if she could. Sliding her cheek over his pelt, Eva could feel him pulsing within, feel the heat rising from him and enveloping her with warmth, such warmth.

The scents of rain and musk were a heady perfume and she pressed her nose close, inhaling his most private scent, even more intoxicating than the fragrance wafting from his skin.

She purred, loving the sound that naturally emerged from her; thrilling to his answering low growl. His hands were in her hair, sifting gently, then insistently pulling her head back until she raised her face to his.

"There's a change coming on me," he said. "What's beneath the surface is close to emerging and once started, I can't stop it. We call it The Unveiling. These are our origins and not even logic can eradicate this stripping of the civilized veneer we hold so tightly to. It's painful for the male, but he has to endure it to prove himself strong enough for his mate. And she has to be strong enough to see his changing—then brave enough to accept him as the beast he is. If you can't bear to be touched by a beast, then tell me now. Tell me before it's too late."

Could she bear it? Eva knew the only thing she couldn't bear would be the loss of their once-in-a-lifetime love.

"I want you, Urich. In any way, shape or form, I want you." Stroking that marvelous lush texture, she could feel he was rigid but sleek beneath. But when she tried to expose him, Urich cinched her wrist and pulled her hand away.

"Careful. Unleash me there and the change will be on me before either of us are ready."

"Will I change, too?" she asked, a little hopefully. There was some comfort in thinking that whatever he became, she would be equal in his prowess.

"Physically?" He shook his head. "You're not genetically able. However..." He looked away. "Your genes are sufficiently compatible to give birth to a hybrid like myself."

Amazingly, it was the first thing he'd said that gave Eva pause. It should be preposterous, worrying about not having any condoms when he was made too uniquely to wear one. But what a serious consideration it was. "We seem to have a problem now. I don't have any birth control."

"It doesn't—" He hesitated, then gestured to his genitals. "If the child could be spared this, if we could live out our days together and raise a family here—would you want my children?"

Wanting to give him the assurance he seemed so needful of, she quickly did so. "I didn't want to have John's babies because something in me insisted that a child deserved two parents who couldn't live without each other. That's the way it is with us. Would I want your children? Yours and only yours, Urich."

His smile was tinged with sorrow. "I just needed to know if you would want what I do, so much, so very much—but can never have." He took a ragged breath, then said, "I'm infertile, Eva. I can mate but I can't breed. We're a dying race, you see. Our ability to propagate was taken from us. Almost."

When she would have asked him more, Urich put a finger to her lips. "Put aside what's better saved for later and take what I offer you now: my mark. It's the sign of my protection, our mutual possession, and once there, it can never be erased. None of my kind would ever dare touch you and no human male who valued his gender would try to steal my claim for as long as I live. Mate with me and those children you wish for might never be. Give your answer with care. You'll never make a decision more binding than this."

Gazing at him, at this child of the universe who had brought such infinite wonder to her life, Eva was moved. That he would bind himself to her, a woman not so different from the others of her world, was testimony to the highest universal truth—the one Everywoman knew from the first breath she took; the one that was rooted in the heart.

"Love, real love, is unconditional, Urich. Love simply is, and the simple truth is—I do love you. You've changed my life and I don't want to live it without you. Children would be icing on the cake, but you're the cake."

There was joy, sheer joy in his kiss. But when he broke it, his voice was somber. "The changing is near and waiting. You're ready for this?"

Upon her nod, Urich softly chanted. He swayed to a ritual sound, an alien incantation spoken in such a way she knew it was holy.

And then he said, "I vow my eternal devotion to you."

"And I give mine to you."

"Ah, Eva, I—" His sudden stillness was absolute; it seemed he was poised, listening for something only he could hear, waiting for something only he could see.

And then he doubled over.

"Urich, Urich, what's wrong, what's—"

"It's happening. Please, Eva, whatever you do, don't run. If you do, I'm afraid that I might—might—attack you."

"I won't run." She reached for him but he staggered back, hugged himself as if trying to contain something that was tearing him apart.

His eyes rolled up. His face contorted in anguish, and how it hurt to see him twisting against the binding of his shirt.

The seams split. The muscles of his chest were expanding before her stricken eyes while her ears registered the ripping of stitches. His sleeves hung in tatters, revealing his biceps, enlarged and rippling with a powerful grace as he tore off the shirt with a chilling howl. Arms reaching for the sky, his hands nearly doubled in size while his fingers curled slightly in and his nails extended into deadly talons.

She couldn't have run if she'd wanted to, so compelling was his wrenching transition. And thank God she couldn't run; his thighs were flexing, extending into powerful pistons of muscle and flesh that could surely overtake her in a single leap.

His gaze that had turned inward now focused on her. His eyes glittered with a ferocious hunger and she heard the snap of bones shifting, saw the slight but noticeable recession of his cheeks, the extension of his jaw, lending him a striking likeness to a wolf.

But it was a man who spoke, his voice a rough, riveting sound that matched his altered physique.

"It's over. Are you afraid of what you see?"

"No." But she should be trembling, terrified by this man-creature who towered over her, majestic and formidable in his brute strength.

"You're very brave. A worthy mate I now claim for my own." A growl emerged from his throat as he stroked a talon over hers. "Bare your neck."

Eva took off her trim jacket. Then, with surprisingly steady hands, she unbuttoned her silk blouse, tossed it beside his shorn shirt. Opening her arms, her mind and emotions, she offered him all that she was, had been, could ever be.

His hair whipped her breasts as he shook his head. "First, I'll hear you ask for my mark."

"Mark me," she whispered, arching her neck.

His head lowered until lightly, ever so lightly, his teeth grazed her skin, made it tingle with anticipation.

"I love you, Eva. And it's with love that I give you the kiss of the beast."

His teeth clamped her neck and she could feel those two sharp incisors lodge there. A shooting pain mingled with an ecstasy rush as his lips yawned wide and his tongue laved her. His jaws—she could feel them working back and forth with the force of his sucking. And his teeth, they were moving all the while, pressing and retreating but never withdrawing from her skin, unmistakable in their coupling intent.

She couldn't move. She couldn't speak. All she could do was accept his possession of the very life of her and exult in his hunger, his mouth drinking her in.

A transcendent kiss of mysterious power was the kiss of the beast. She was floating, and if this was death, then how sweet to die, to trip on the light fantastic, her body electric with the fusion of their souls.

His teeth slipped from her neck and only then did she cry out: "Don't stop! Come back. Urich, come back!"

"It's done," he pronounced gravely. And then he put his predator's hand to her throat. He could have torn it open with a single swipe to her jugular, but no greater protection had she ever felt than in his moving caress, which imparted a glowing sensation.

"I've sealed the wounds, but my mark is forever. Not even time, in all its fickle composition, can erase my eternal kiss. You trusted me with the life I've vowed to honor above my own. In exchange, I give the life in me, to you."

The bed sank almost to the floor as he settled his weight on the edge and pulled her onto his lap. It felt like the size of a throne, his groin a cushion that was softer than silk, harder than jutting granite.

He urged her head to his shoulder but Eva pulled away, held his brutally beautiful face in her hands. "What you did was...a wondrous thing and...and I want you to do it again. Again and again. But, Urich, I can't do that to you."

"You think I want you to mark me?" At her nod, he chuckled. "You'll mark me as yours, but not with your teeth."

"Then...how?"

He smiled with a dark radiance, wolverine incisors tipped with a moonlight sheen. "We mate."

It's savage and it's sacred. Eva, I cannot. She'd thought many times of those words framing his refusal, and with great curiosity; but now that the moment was at hand, she wondered if curiosity could indeed kill the cat.

"Will you hurt me?"

"Hurt what I would die to protect?" He licked her neck. "This is the sign of my protection—even from me. Had you run before I marked you...I shudder to think. But you didn't, just as I knew you wouldn't. Eva," he said with great pride, "you did well. There's not another in the universe more courageous than you."

She did feel courageous. Courageous and proud to bear Urich's sign of their bond. She also felt worthy of it, equal to his awesome strength. There was no fear in her, none at all. It made her a little reckless, induced her to ask, "So I'm safe...even if I run?"

"Oh, I'd like that. Especially since you probably wouldn't be an easy catch. Listen, can you hear her?"

A distant sound, she heard it. Closer it came until she knew that if only she reached within, she could race the wind, touch the stars, be anything she imagined she could be.

A feline smile tilted her lips. "The lioness."

"Yes-s-s," he hissed.

Although she experienced no physical changes such as his, there was a change working in her, too. Her sense of self was crystallizing as never before, gathering momentum and being infused with so much energy that her limbs twitched with the need to release it. Had his bite done this? Or had her show of courage been the catalyst that finally unleashed the wildish woman she no longer feared.

Skating a nail over his enormous chest, Eva murmured, "So what's a lioness to do on her mating night?"

His lip lifted in a sexy snarl. "She runs with the wolf."

"Or..." Bounding from his lap, Eva stretched enticingly, then leaped away from his possessive snatch at her. "She could run from him."

His laughter was more a low growl. "There's not much sport to be had here. Come with me, Eva. Let's go to a special world, a place that's untouched by time."

Unable to resist, she took his hand. A whirling white light surrounded them, mingled with a clamorous noise, then spinning, spinning them. The breath was sucked from her lungs and then returned with a whoosh that nearly burst them.

Holding on for dear life to his waist, she waited for the dizziness to pass, certain she must be imagining a place so far beyond beautiful that it had to be heaven.

But no, she was steady now and blinking against a pristine sky so blue it was almost blinding. The sound of nature was all around her, singing in harmony like the universe. Her feet were planted on grass, each blade glistening emerald. Nearby, a crystal waterfall cascaded over skyscraper rocks; even the water sang. It joined the humming leaves dancing upon a boundless vista of trees. From waving branches, lush, ripe fruit bobbed in delectable hues.

"Is this Eden?" she whispered.

"Just as beautiful and just as wrathful if adulterated. These are hallowed grounds, a honeymoon spot of sorts for my people. It's been a long time since anyone's visited here. We won't be disturbed."

He rubbed sinuously against her. A nip to her bottom lip and he led her to stroke his arousal.

One that was large enough to make running seem wise.

"You, ah, seem to have grown there, too." Aware that her touching was increasing his excitement and her apprehension in equal degrees, Eva patted his chest and took a step back.

Urich's advance matched her retreat. His frown held a hint of amusement. "What's this? You're suddenly nervous, now that I'm the one who's ready to mate? Maybe I should entice you with a few of those little tortures you were so generous in doling out to me."

Eva gulped dry air. "Maybe you're ready, but I'm not."

"So it seems. But once you're closer to nature, the rest is sure to follow." In a blur of swipes, he had her naked. Stepping back to assess his handiwork, Urich said with approval, "Much better."

Her body responded to the wisp of nirvana air swirling over her, his scent tantalizing her senses. But still . . .

"A woman likes to be romanced, and stripping her in a matter of seconds is *not* romantic," she told him.

"Romance? I'll give you your night in white satin—at another time and in another place. But this first time, in this place, we mate my way."

It's sacred and it's savage. Taking in the formidable proportions of him, the simmer of his gaze fixed on the apex of her thighs, Eva wondered just how savage he might get. The haven of her bedroom had provided a sense of security, and she had teased him to chase her there.

But this was his turf and Urich was serious in his intent to have at it in no tame way.

He took a menacing step forward, which she followed with two steps back. "I'm not ready."

"Then do your best to escape the inevitable." Hunkering down, poised to lunge, he was in midair when she took off.

17

URICH LANDED NEATLY on all fours. Watching her streak toward the refuge of untamed woodlands, he chuckled. Maybe Eva was more Deducian than not, her flight-for-life instinct a most logical reaction.

As for him, he had new appreciation for his heritage. Liberated from the mask of civility, the beast within was a free, stalking creature who was one with nature, and with himself.

Soon he would be one with his mate.

But not too soon. He wanted Eva's own civilized veneer gone by the time he caught her. And then he wanted nothing less than for them to forge a pact that stripped them down to their very bones in an act of utter surrender and raw passion.

How limited humans were in their definition of romance. Eva saw as others did not; she would see the stark romance of relinquishing the fetters of restraint.

She would see the binding grace and honesty that came from embracing the animal within them both.

HER HEART BEAT IN TIME to her racing feet. The landscape streaked by in a blur of rampant color. Whether her lightning speed was owed to this unearthly Eden, to Urich's bite, or to adrenaline, Eva didn't know. Nor did she care.

For now, all that mattered was leading Urich on this cat-and-mouse chase until he wore himself out, looking for her.

That could be a very long time.

Flying past trees and flowers and lakes, she was aware they possessed a preternatural beauty that echoed Urich's own. She felt like a wood nymph herself, with breasts swinging freely, tickled by the gentle, sweet-fragranced wind; her feet caressed by velvety grass; her thighs lightly brushing as they pumped in exhilarated abandon.

She could see for miles, hear every bird, every rustle of a leaf; smell the plenitude of nature, the richness of soil and dew-kissed air.

She felt as free and untamed as the refuge that beckoned.

A sly smile sparked her lips. She'd doubled back; returned to the haven of a waterfall she'd spied earlier.

Her feet were sure as she leaped from rock to rock at the bottom, and took the path that led to a hidden cave. Cascading water draped its entrance and although she knew she should hide in the darkness beyond, the temptation to linger won out.

A fine, cool spray drizzled over her and she gave in to the luxury of its sensual caress. The rainbow of mist soothed her flushed face, sifted over her neck. She raised her arms and water trickled down them and sheened her breasts. Cupping them, she lifted them closer to the spray, which tantalized her nipples.

Never had she felt so heavenly hedonistic, so at one with nature and with herself. Eva tossed her head in sweeping, uninhibited arcs until her hair streamed out in wild disarray.

She slid her fingertips over her belly and the curves of her hips, then rounded her breasts. Tracing the two small crescents on her neck, she considered the magnitude of their meaning.

The kiss of the beast was the equivalent of a wedding ring. But while rings and the vows they signified could be discarded, Urich had made it clear only death could break them apart. Eva indulged in a smirk.

He had to learn that this was one mate who bowed to no man's rule and she didn't come on demand, in bed or out.

Wolf he might be, but she had outwitted him. Still gloating, she turned. And stopped in mid-step.

"In all worthy matches, a pitting of wiles and wills is necessary to discover who's the stronger and ultimately leads." His voice echoed from wall to wall, snaked through her head in a seductive whisper.

A gust of air assaulted her with his seductive scent, sapping her will to escape the magnificent beast who loomed in the shadows.

"It's not fair," she protested, even as she gravitated to his hulking presence. "Luring me isn't fair."

"All's fair in love and war, as your people say." He stepped from the shadows and into the light. "My people make love and war at once with their mates. *War with me.* Either war with me or give yourself to me, as I'll have you anyway in the end."

Closing the distance in a single leap, he grabbed her, turned her around and bent her over. Eva jerked free and bared her teeth, then raised her hand in a clawing threat. His playful swatting away of her dubious weapon and his indulgent laughter, infuriated her.

Urich wanted a war? She'd give him Armageddon!

In a single swipe her nails streaked across his chest. His growl of delight maddened her, excited her, and she hurled herself at him with such force that his back hit the cave's smooth stone floor. Rising atop him, she knew a moment's victory and crowed in primal triumph.

With a roar, he tossed her off. They circled each other like two jungle cats sizing each other up, both of them determined to lead the pack.

She feinted a knee to his groin, which he instantly covered. Seizing the advantage, Eva swept a foot behind his.

Down he went—only to latch onto her ankle and yank her to the ground before she could retreat.

They grappled and wrestled and rolled, each fighting for supremacy over the other. A part of her knew he was infinitely stronger, that he could have finished their struggle quickly. But this seemed to be an alien sort of foreplay; his enjoyment of it evident in his light pawing of her breasts, his legs slipping and sliding around hers, his arousal brushing her amid their tussle.

She was aroused. Eva was ready to mount him herself when he put a sudden end to their wrestling. He caught her flailing fists, raised them high above her head.

The flush of his passion was as dark as it was deep.

So, too, was his demand: "Submit. Submit to me."

She wanted his possession, and yet she was still flush with the fight in this battle of wills. "No."

"Then I'll just have to persuade you." One vibrating touch to her cleft left her gasping, ready to agree to anything, everything, but she couldn't draw breath to say so.

His own breath was moving from her neck to her breasts, then hot and moist on her belly. And then it was between her thighs, joined with the sweep of his tongue. He bathed her with languorous licks that moved ever closer to his massaging fingertip. And then his tongue was there, lapping and making her writhe as he whispered against her, "Sweet, so sweet and delicious. I can't get enough."

Something slipped inside her and swirled, moving up and up until she felt a tingling flick at the tip of her womb.

Amid her mindless cries of delirious pleasure, she realized it was his tongue laving her.

"I can't stand it anymore!" she finally shrieked, gripping him by his hair and pulling, tearing at it until he had no choice but to stop or lose his mane to her frenzied hands.

"So wet," he murmured, brushing his lips against hers. "Soft and clutching. Nectar to the tongue." His smile was tender. "Submit to me, Eva." Then, as if sharing a secret that would bind them, he whispered, "Submit to me and become the stronger. Make me weak with the strength of your submission."

More an entreaty than a command, she had no will or want to resist. She offered her throat to him, arching her neck in glad defeat. He bit it softly until she moaned for more.

"Then take more," he murmured. From his sumptuous cloak emerged a rigid sleekness that he slid between her legs. Like a moist tongue in texture, but it was unmistakably a penis testing her entry with a smooth, easy rhythm.

"The mating dance of nature, Eva," he roughly crooned. "Come dance with me and meet my strength."

She let him turn her over, guide her palms to the floor, arms braced. He roamed her belly, lifted her hips with a cinching hold. Stepping with her knees, spreading them apart, she enticed him with the swish of her buttocks to his groin.

His thighs came over hers and rocked. Back and forth he rocked until she was impatient with his slow, sustained pace.

"You're teasing me," she said, wanting more than a minuet and gyrating her hips in rumba fashion.

"I'm making you want the ride." Thighs strapping tighter over hers, he rendered her still while his nails streaked lightly over her back. Up and down, rivulets of prickling sensation following their path and making her buck like a mare against the saddle of his stern hold.

"Ride me!" she cried.

He met her demand with a small, initial breach that left her gasping, then seemingly endless was his smooth glide. She felt him expanding with a magnitude that left no room for even the slightest friction.

His breath hot and searingly near, he gritted out, "We're locked. This is how we stay until your release releases me. Now I submit to serving your ultimate pleasure." His teeth clamped through her hair and pinched her nape.

The paralysis. It was the same inability to move, to speak, to do anything but breathe that had overcome her on the terrace. But she had been alone then, and now she was being taken with a silent ferocity.

It was an eloquent ravishing: She could feel the brush of mink slapping against her buttocks as he humped her. But inside, they were locked as surely as one entity of flesh.

They pulsed in a singular, meltingly warm ache. In her mind she saw him on her, the two of them like animals in heat, and she was thrilling to his dominion while holding him enslaved to the release she struggled to deny herself, wanting their imprisonment to this ecstasy without end.

The prison was too savagely sweet, stunning in the spiral of sensation it created. Her release ripped through her with a convulsive ferocity. His teeth left her nape. Freed from his pinioning hold, she gave a keening wail and thrashed wildly beneath him.

With an urgent jerk, he lifted her hips. And then he was moving in and out of her with a sleek friction that took her on wave upon wave of a rapacious coming and coming again.

His breath, a sequence of labored grunts, ended with a final, jolting plunge. Liquid heat flooded her, filled her and streamed between her legs.

Urich collapsed. Just when Eva was certain that what was left of her would be crushed under his weight, she heard the retreating beat of a war drum. His heart was the sound of that drum; slowing, fading, she could feel it against her back. His thighs quivered over her trembling ones. A low howl accompanied the shift of his body's structure in a reverse transformation.

What was in her retracted, slipping out as easily as a snake shedding its skin.

"No, no," she whimpered. Reaching for what she was loathe to give up, her palm wrapped around his sheath. Just as luxurious, just as tempting to wallow in.

He was flaccid beneath.

His hand came over hers and she felt licks, loving wet licks to her back. "Beauty, you conquered the beast. Brought him to heel with your acceptance, mastered him with a strength beyond his own."

"I wish him back already," Eva said, her sense of loss making her voice catch. "I really do adore my Beast."

"That's good to hear since he definitely adores you." Richly laughing, Urich pulled her into his arms, stroked her hair while she nuzzled against his chest. "I'm sure you could induce him to do an encore. He's not a sore loser."

Draping a leg over his, Eva winced. She was sore, marvelously so, and so wondrously replete on this cave floor misted with a rainbow spray, that she decided, "Maybe he should take a rest. As for me, I could die happy just like this. I've never felt so at peace and that's a little amazing to me. So savage, but I feel so whole. How can that be?"

"Look within," he coaxed. "Your answer lies there."

Look she did and what Eva saw was a very simple truth— one that Urich had shared before but only now did she grasp.

"There *is* an animal in all of us. You weren't the only beast I accepted. I accepted the one in myself."

"Yes."

And then she realized something else, and that something was a little scary. "We could tear each other apart, Urich."

"With our wiles and wills, we could easily do just that. But we're smart animals, Eva, smart enough to respect the worthiness of our match." With a lusty growl, he concluded,

"And what a match you are. I'll have to choose my wars with you carefully or chance losing them every time."

It wasn't the stuff of sweet murmurings and proclamations of love in the aftermath of passion spent. But she thought Urich's blunt appraisal of their uncivil bond an expression of intimacy that was honest, rare. And *very* romantic.

"Know what?" she purred. "Cary Grant could take lessons from you."

18

"KISS ME?" EVA ASKED in the midst of their lazy bath.

Treading the waterfall pool, Urich eagerly bent to take more than a turn at rubbing rose petals in her hair.

Water rushed up into his face and Eva giggled as she made a hasty retreat. She was a better swimmer than he and gained land before he could do more than sputter, "Come back!"

Laughing gaily, she took off for the woods, taunting, "Catch me if you can!"

By the time he did, she gave him a kiss to make up for her trickery. Reveling in their natural states and in each other, they romped and strolled, laughed and shared easy silences in this timeless place.

How he longed to stay here forever, never to return to reality. Even to think of it was to taint the ethereal moment they shared as Eva held a persimmon to his lips. But just as he started to take a bite, reality reared its serpent head, stealing away their time even here.

"We have to go," he said, anxiety sharpening his command. "Now, Eva. *Now.* Hold tight to me."

"But—"

He seized her to him and could only pray his sense of direction steered them home. His mind was where he had left it: Behind. With Zar.

Thankfully, they arrived where they'd departed from— Eva's bedroom. Her room where time had stood still and it was nudging midnight; all was the same but nothing was the same at all. Not them, not his rude jolt of near discovery and the severe consequences it would have wrought. From here to eternity and back, how greatly things had changed.

"Why did we have to leave?" she asked, still breathless from their swift departure and almost immediate return.

Tell her, he silently ordered himself. *She has to know why you marked her in such haste, what the result of it could be. Just tell her the whole, ugly truth.*

"An intruder was coming," he replied stiffly. "I was wrong about us not being disturbed."

Eva flinched and he released her from his harsh grip. He couldn't look at her and hide his rage, his distress. Urich went to her closet and tossed her a robe.

"What's the matter?" she demanded. "One minute we're lovers in Nirvana and the next we're here and you won't say why, except that we were about to be disturbed. *I'm* disturbed. Something's wrong and I want to know what it is."

"We didn't have the proper permission to be there." That much was true. "And I didn't want him to see you naked." Very, very true.

"Him? How did you know it was a guy?"

"I sensed—" Urich swallowed against the words clogged in his throat "—my father."

"Your father! Couldn't you have gotten my clothes and introduced us? I really would have liked to meet him."

"But I don't want him to meet you."

Eva looked hurt. And then, indignant. "Why? Are you ashamed of me? Is there some kind of stigma attached to pairing up with an Earthling?"

"That's ridiculous. I'm a hybrid myself and infinitely prouder of you than Zar ever was of my mother."

"So, dear old Dad has a name. But that still doesn't explain why you don't want me to meet him. If you're not ashamed of me, then what gives?"

"What gives is that he might be my biological father but he is no 'Dad' to me." Although Zar couldn't help what he was, Urich felt resentment rise as he explained, "A dad shows affection—a concept Deducians can't grasp. Perhaps I can because I'm not pure. Zar is. Only twice has he ever touched me. Once, to strike me when I jeered at the emptiness of logic being all there was to existence. I was a child then, and quickly learned my value was based on my abilities and they were only as good as the service I put them to. The other contact came much later. He expressed his pride in my service and hugged me. An embarrassing episode for us both."

"That's—that's— Urich, that's horrible." She hugged him so fiercely that it seemed she was trying to give him all the hugs he'd missed as a child. "How horrible for you to be raised with that kind of emotional neglect. It's criminal."

"From your perspective, yes. But yours isn't theirs. They don't know any better, not even Zar, and no blame can be put on them for being what they simply are."

"Call me human, but I blame them plenty and you have every right to blame them even more."

"Do I?" Urich disentangled her arms and held her slightly away. "When I first came to you, I was more like them than not." Worse than they were, he had been ambitious—his intent to manipulate Eva to his advantage so he might prove his value beyond dispute.

"But that wasn't your fault," she insisted. "They made you like them. But you're not one of them anymore."

She was right about that. And he was human enough to want those excuses she was making for his coldhearted plans that had turned on him with a cruel vengeance.

Now was the time to expose himself as the imposter he was. Eva's mood was one of sympathy and she still wore the glow of their intimate bonding. He could better woo her understanding now than at a moment when she could examine more clearly the situation he was responsible for.

Urich snorted in self-derision. Here he went again, trying to manipulate her emotions to his advantage.

"I'm still enough like them to bear the mark of the beast and share it with you." Scowling darkly, he set her away. "And there's enough of Zar in me to need some distance from these cloying emotions."

"Cloying?" she repeated, her face filled with hurt. But then she lifted up her chin and thumped his chest. "Fine for you, but what about me? I need to be touched. I need to express what I feel and have some feelings returned from you. *What are you feeling?*"

Guilty. Cornered. Ashamed. Loved.

"I'm sorry, Eva, but I feel claustrophobic." Afraid of gripping her to him and pouring out all that he truly did feel, Urich stepped beyond her reach. "I'll be back. Right now I just need some time alone."

"After—after everything we've..." At his nod, she snapped, "You want your space? You've got it. As far as I'm concerned you can go to hell, and the hell I care if you never come back, you—you alien!"

He deserved it, every scathing word. But jagged as his edges were, he gave in to the need to vent them on the one soul he loved. "Don't *ever* speak to me like that again. I won't tolerate such lack of respect from anyone, but especially not from you. My mark is on you and the beast who put it there would rather take you to hell with him than burn without his mate. Remember that before you spout such garbage again."

She swiped at her neck as if trying to erase the irrevocable. "Then take your mark back. I won't be stuck with any man who acts like he's lord and master over me."

"Lest you forget, I'm not a man," he said with coldness to her heated rebuke. Thrusting aside her agitated fingertips, he possessively stroked his thumb over the mark. "And lest you forget, I warned you of the significance of this. Still, you asked for The Kiss. Too late, Eva, you *are* stuck with that decision and the beast you took for a mate."

Before he marked her again for good measure, Urich turned on his heel. Several paces down the hallway and he heard the door slam—then slam again. No knob. And he wouldn't be fixing it, either, since she'd probably lock him out the next time they had a battle of wills.

Eva's was strong and gaining strength. He had met his match, indeed. Urich smiled grimly, realizing he'd rather be fighting with her than closeting himself in this spare room to restore his clothing and give some perspective to his thoughts.

With that perspective came the hard facts: Life with Eva could have ended already, had Zar come upon them. Zar, who had decided to visit the grounds he was anticipating using himself. And so eager for it, he'd come to see the lay of the land where he'd exult in serving his ultimate purpose.

Traitor that he himself had turned, Urich found his only comfort in knowing that he'd given Eva a protective stay from the very thing he had targeted her for. *Could it get any worse?*

Oh, yes. Much worse. What just cause she would have to despise him for all that he'd done—for all that could still happen to her, should he meet his end.

How very precious their time together was; and yet he had divided them with this distance and words that had bitten her more sharply than his teeth.

She was surely nursing the wounds he had inflicted by putting his need to brood alone above her need for togetherness. The right thing to do was to make amends as best he could. Again. With a weary sigh, he wondered how his mind could work so quickly only to be such a slow learner when it came to knowing what really counted—the heart.

His own was heavy as he went to her room. Which was empty.

Hardly surprising. But then she surprised him, as she so often did, by calling from the balcony, "I'm out here."

EVA CHAFED HER ARMS against the chill of night, the fever in her heart. She didn't want this need for his touch, but when his hand came over hers, she took its comfort and said quietly, "I never want to suffocate you and if that's how you were feeling, then you were right to say so."

"Why are you being so kind?"

"Because I can either stay mad and make us both miserable or let it go—the way I should have let you go instead of lashing out at you because—"

"I deserved it. Eva, I'm sorry, so sorry for ruining what was meant to be a night as special as you are to me." He laced his fingers with hers, squeezed. "It wasn't you I needed to get away from, but a wedge that's between my father and me. Why I struck out at you when I prize you above life itself, that's a mystery to me. Maybe it springs from those emotions I'm still trying to master."

"Those emotions you're trying to master are the ones that enslave us all." She turned her puffy but now dry eyes to his. "It's an irony of life that people tend to take out their frustrations on those they love the most."

Ever so tender was his kiss to each eyelid before he said, "You've been crying."

"Tears are cleansing and crying made me feel better." She smiled wryly. "Almost as good as tearing up what was left of your shirt before I threw your pants over the balcony while I consigned you and Walt Disney both to hell."

"Walt Disney? Didn't he make your favorite movie?"

"Sure, *Peter Pan*. But mad as I was, I told him all his happily-ever-afters were a crock of shit. And he could put his fairy dust . . . well, where the crock got its contents."

Urich's laughter rolled out across the sky. "My old home seems about as close as Never-Never Land from here. But this is where the real magic is, not there . . . Wendy. That's who you remind me of. Wise beyond your years and yet there's enough of the girl in you to still believe in magic."

Eva wrinkled her nose. "I'd rather be Tinker Bell. She's the one with all the fairy dust."

Chuckling, Urich pressed a kiss to her palm, then folded in her fingers. "Go ahead. Throw it."

Her palm tingled and ebullient laughter bubbled from her throat. She felt as if she held every joy in the world in her hand, and how tempting it was to keep all that joy for herself.

But joy, like magic and love, was only good when it was shared. Eva made a silent wish for all three to sweep the world as she cast them to the wind to land where they might.

HIS HOPE WAS SOARING higher by the minute. Watching Raven preen under Justine's toying attentions to his mane of silver hair, Urich patted Eva's knee. She nudged him in the ribs and whispered, "What do you think?"

"It's going better than good," he whispered back, taking note of Raven's broad smile across the pub table. "He seems to like nachos and cola almost as much as he likes Justine."

"She sure seems to like him." When Justine slid onto his lap, Eva added, "Maybe a little too much?"

A full day spent showing Raven a good time and Urich was needful of more than his discreet touching of Eva, who was ever so careful not to raise suspicion about what the long crimson scarf on her neck concealed. But if snuggling was okay for Raven, they could certainly do the same.

Pulling Eva onto his lap, Urich murmured, "Like me too much, too."

"I do," she assured him, cuddling close and giggling when he playfully nipped her ear.

"Eva," Raven said suddenly, "Justine tells me that your scarf gives her some naughty ideas. I haven't been able to guess what those might be, but she says if you'll loan your scarf to us, she'll give me a little demonstration."

Urich stiffened; so did Eva. He'd told her Raven would be upset if he saw the mark. As for why, she'd accepted his explanation that he'd forgone the Tribunal's blessing—a gross breach of protocol he'd clear up later. So wrapped up in the splendor of their insular world, he'd almost convinced himself that love would find a way to overcome any and all obstacles, just as Eva had assured him it would.

"Uh...here?" she asked uneasily. "Justine, don't you think a private place would be better?"

"Oh, c'mon, nobody'll notice." She indicated the barrel chair's wood arm. "Let us have some fun."

"Yes, fun!" Raven concurred. Then to Urich, he said, "This fun I'm having is all that you promised it would be. Eva is delightful. Justine is—" he leaned across the table and growled "—M-m-marvelous. The food is—out of this world!" Raven laughed at his own wit while Urich forced a strained chuckle. "I could stay here forever."

Urich subdued a groan. His plan to introduce Raven to Earth's pleasures was backfiring. Hell and be damned, what *hadn't* backfired since he'd first met Eva in the holodeck?

"Much as we'd like you to stay, aren't you forgetting your meeting with our boss?" he pointedly reminded. "He is expecting you for dinner, and we do need to discuss a few details before you go."

Raven scowled, looking as though the prospect of consuming tasteless protein and bland liquid nourishment held no more appeal than reporting to Zar.

"Of course," he grumbled. Urich breathed a sigh of relief, then cringed when Raven brightened, saying, "All the more reason to have this naughty bit of fun before I go." He held out his hand to Eva. "Please, might we borrow your scarf? You've been such a generous and lovely creature, and I'd be most appreciative if you'd indulge me with this."

In Eva's ear, Urich sharply commanded, *"Don't."*

Her gaze darted nervously from him to Raven's waiting palm. "I—I'm sorry, but I've got...a cold." She sneezed. "I'm wearing it to keep away the draft."

"What draft?" Justine asked, fanning herself. "It's too hot in here, if you ask me. Then again, it could just be what all this silver hair does to me."

"His hair! Good idea, Justine. Use his hair." Eva wrapped a stream of Urich's around her wrist.

Raven's shrewd gaze fixed on Eva's neck. "Odd that you developed such a sudden cold," he observed, all play gone from his tone. His eyes cut a severe path to Urich's, which were filled with dread. "But given the condition you're in, keep the scarf where it is. If you'll excuse me, I need to visit the...men's room. Why don't you come with me, Urich? We can discuss our business in there."

Raven nearly dumped Justine on the floor as he stood. Back rigid, he stalked away like a general marching to a war.

Urich held Eva close, gathering what strength he could as he said quietly, "Once we're alone, we have to talk."

"I want to talk now. What's going on?"

A nightmare. A catastrophe. He couldn't even begin to describe the devastation about to rip their world to shreds.

"This won't take long. What I have to say to you, will. Raven's waiting. I have to go."

When she didn't budge, Urich returned her to the chair he wanted to send flying through the room, took a bracing drink before returning his glass to the table he wanted to shatter with his fist, then turned toward the fate awaiting him.

Stiffly, he forced his feet forward like a stoic soldier approaching the noose that was waiting to hang him.

Eva watched him go while a sick, sick feeling twisted her stomach.

"Gee, that's kinda weird," Justine remarked. "I thought women were the only ones who went to the bathroom together."

19

"*YOU MARKED HER.*" Raven's livid glare could have cut a diamond. "How could you commit such a crime?"

"How could I not?" Urich retorted. "It's the only protection I could give Eva and that's a reason more sacred than Zar's mark could ever be. He won't touch her now—not for as long as I'm alive."

"For as long as you're alive?" Raven scoffed. "You've all but sealed your death warrant. And possibly mine. Zar won't forgive this humiliation you've dealt him, and well he shouldn't. How can a ruler rule when his son does worse than spit in his face, and in such a public way?"

The door swung open and a patron entered a nearby stall. Lowering his voice to a whisper, Urich argued, "No one knows other than you."

"Not yet. But Zar has to know the mate he's expecting won't be delivered as you promised, and duty decrees that he keep nothing of significance from the Tribunal. *This is significant.* What help I could have given you is gone, Urich. They'll have a full accounting from us both and honor demands that I expose the information I never should have withheld." Raven shook his head in bewilderment. "Why, *why* did I stay silent when I could have stopped this before it went beyond damage control?"

"You stayed silent because it was the right thing to do." Urich gripped his friend's slumped shoulder and said firmly, "Because you are and always have been more of a father to me than Zar was capable of being. I wish I were your son,

Raven. And I wish that we could both stay in this world forever. We could have some great fun, eh?"

"Yes, well..." Raven cleared his throat awkwardly and just as awkwardly patted Urich's hand before removing it from the shoulder he straightened. "Unfortunately, wishing won't change anything. We'll face them together, Urich. And we'll accept whatever befalls us with the honor we'll likely take to our graves. Agreed?"

Urich nodded, although in his heart he knew his own tarnished honor would rebel against the fate he was sure to be dealt.

"Prepare the assembly for my return. I'll appear after I speak with Eva. I dread that even more than the high court. While I should regret all that I've done, there's no regret in me for loving her, despite its price."

"She's all that you say she is, Urich. Had I been you, I would have lost my reason, too...son." With that blessing of understanding, Raven said, "Please give my regrets to Justine for leaving to see to more pressing matters."

"Of course." Urich proffered his right hand, which Raven readily shook. "I'll see you. Soon."

Raven gave a short bow and was gone, his departure coinciding with the flush of a toilet.

Urich thought it an apt summation of the future he had seen and discounted as too fantastical to believe. A future that was sucking him downward even now. And not even fairy dust could change it.

"WHY DID YOU WANT to talk here?" Eva asked nervously in the rain-forest setting of the holodeck.

"Because this is where we started." The bleakness of his tone implied that it was also where they would part.

"You're scaring me, Urich. Why did Raven leave? Why do I get the really horrible feeling that you're getting ready to leave yourself? And that—that whatever it is you said we have to talk about is going to be worse than horrible?"

"It is." He took her trembling hand and her anxiety grew closer to terror; he was shaking, too. "There's no way I can soften the harshness of the truth I should never have hidden from you. But I did, Eva. I was human enough to lie to myself and to you. A lie of omission but a lie just the same."

"This isn't happening," she whispered, wanting to cover her ears and not hear any more. "I'm having a nightmare and I'm going to wake up and you'll be there holding me and telling me I had a bad dream, that everything's all right."

"Nothing is all right. Everything is wrong." He took a deep breath while she couldn't get enough air past the constriction of her lungs. "When I first came to you, my purpose was to win your trust. A trust you gave and I didn't deserve. My only hope is that I can spare you the reason I was sent here— to fulfill a role in a very important mission."

Eva willed herself to hear him out and stay as calm as she could. She had to stay calm to think and she had to think of some way to keep him. "What—what mission, Urich?"

"To bring you willingly to my people. And once there, to assist us with a capability you possess but we lack."

"Emotions?" His silence was a dread sound. "Look, if you need me to help your people get in touch with their feelings so they can adapt to Earth, no problem. Sign me up, take me with you. I'll be glad to go."

"No," he said flatly. "If you go, it won't be a better understanding of emotions they'll want from you."

Her heart on hold, she asked, "What would they want me for?"

"To breed."

Stunned beyond speech, all she could do was stare at him.

"I told you we're a dying race." His voice held a numb quality, as if he were trying to dull the razor about to slice them apart. "What I didn't say was that when we were overtaken, only our elderly females were left. All others were given a choice to be extinguished or sterilized, then sent to serve our enemies. My mother chose to be extinguished."

"And your father let her do it?" she gasped. "Even if he didn't love her, didn't he at least try to fight for her?"

Urich shook his head. "It was a bloodless coup. Logic dictates that it's senseless to kill and be killed in return. Returning war for war wasn't considered a viable option."

"So the males just sat back and let it all happen? What a bunch of gutless wonders," Eva spat with distaste. "But you're different. You would have fought for me."

"I would give my life for you, Eva." There was such certainty in his vow that she was well and truly alarmed. "Now. Or then. How long ago it was, but our present is linked with those past events."

"Go on," she made herself say.

"We made a pact with our adversaries that allowed us to remain on our planet until our race deceased naturally. An inevitability, with all of us sterilized—save one. They believed the remains found were those of our ruler. He still lives...with his fertility intact." Urich drew a ragged breath. "I was to bring you to him."

Eva's voice sounded raw as she struggled to ask, "But why me? Why me, when there's surely a universe of females that are just as fertile?"

"Genetic compatibility, superior intelligence, and many other factors elevated you above the other candidates. Even the ruler can have only one mate, and you were selected as the most qualified. You were the logical choice."

She was hearing it, every toneless word he said, but she couldn't believe a single syllable of it. "Selected as the most qualified? Was I supposed to be flattered that my name was drawn from some sort of computerized gene pool and I got picked to get pregnant because I was the 'logical choice'?"

"It was hoped that...that once I won your agreement, you would consider it an honor to aid our cause. The offspring would be hybrids, but by propagating there was a chance we could remain in our homeland. And if we were displaced, at least the progeny might survive on Earth, even if the rest of us couldn't." His eyes begged her sympathy. "Please, Eva, try to understand."

"I'm trying." But try as she might, she couldn't get past the cowardice that had allowed their females to be so abused. And now, this ruler who had escaped the fate of their women, wanted her to give them some babies. Love had nothing to do with it and no big surprise that was, since Urich's people were as emotionally sterile as their reproductive organs.

How could they think she would allow any children of hers to grow up amid the coldness Urich had been subjected to? Even their approach to selecting and obtaining her was cold.

The only credit she could give them was for wanting her to come willingly—but that smacked of being self-serving, too. After all, if she tried to do herself in like Mylar, or decided she'd rather castrate their ruler in his sleep than get raped by a beast, they'd be better off without her.

"Let me tell you something, Urich. As far as I can see, your species has no one but themselves to blame for the jam they're in, and this plan to get out of it stinks." With a snort of disgust, she demanded, "Who thought it up? The ruler?"

"No." There was a long, foreboding pause. "Me."

Her heart twisted as his revelation sank in. Urich, not only the instrument of her capture, but the instigator of it? If only he had been under orders, been as much a pawn as she; but no, he'd come to her under false pretenses that *he* had devised; had deceived her with a plan of *his* making.

"Eva, please, say something. Yell at me, accuse me, strike me, forgive me, I don't care. Just talk to me."

"How could you?"

Urich flinched. Her whisper was worse than a scream, the tears she held at bay more lashing than a torrent of epithets. And her jerk from his beseeching touch, a rejection more powerful than a slap to his face. The controlled facade he'd struggled to maintain crumpled like brittle paper in the fist she clenched to her breast as she whispered again, "How could you have done this to me, Urich?"

"I couldn't now, Eva, believe me, I couldn't," he said in a passionate rush, unable to bear parting with this between them. "You've changed me from what I was—ambitious and unfeeling and knowing nothing of love. The trap I laid may have been meant for you, but it's me who got caught. Can you find it in your heart to forgive the unforgivable? Even a little?"

His plea mingled with her hurt, so palpable he could feel it. His own hurt went just as deep for being the inflictor of hers and for the first time in his life, Urich wanted to weep. He swallowed against a knot of tears, but couldn't hold back the single, sharp sob that caught in his throat.

It seemed to release the floodgates of Eva's compassion. She grasped his hand, kissed it. "Real love forgives, Urich, and my love for you is unshakable, as certain as the law of nature itself. I forgive you. But we have some damage done that's not going to mend overnight."

"There won't—" He could hardly get the words out. "There won't be time for any mending. Raven left to prepare the Tribunal for my return. Chances are next to none that I'll be back, since the charges I have to face are severe."

"No." She shook her head, shook and shook it as if a swarm of bees were killing her alive with their sting. "No, no, no, no . . ."

"Listen to me!" His fingers dug into her shoulders with an urgency to match the caution she had to hear. "The only fear I have is for you, once my claim is gone."

"But—but you said not even time could erase your mark," she said frantically. "That it's an eternal kiss."

"It is." His stroke to her neck was full of tender possession and ache, so much ache. "But once I die, another can have you. By marking you to protect you from the very thing I targeted you for, I've committed an unpardonable crime. All but Raven will lack any understanding of it—and powerful as his position is, he'll be implicated as an accessory and suffer the consequences of my actions. So I've betrayed not only you, but Raven, as well."

Clutching at him for support, she begged, "Tell me—tell me that you're not up for execution and Raven along with you, because we fell in love."

"That's exactly what I'm telling you. Now, there's one way I might be able to keep you safe, and I think it'll work." *Let it work*, he silently prayed. But if his plan went the way of his botched others... "If it doesn't, then be wary. The one you were intended for could order your abduction."

"Just let him try," she suddenly seethed, the lioness roaring to life and consuming her panic with a white-hot rage. *Good*. Gone he might be, but Eva would still be formidable in her strength. "I'll cut the balls off that bastard if he lays a hand on me. And I'll stab him in the heart he hasn't got if he touches so much as a single hair on you or Raven."

"Brave and worthy as you are, Eva, you would be no match against him," he warned. "Should you present any threat, he'd have your irrationality extracted. A lobotomy to render you incapable of anything except conception."

Fire flashed in her eyes as she demanded, "Just who the hell is this sorry son of a bitch who calls himself a ruler over a bunch of walking-talking computers just like him?"

His smile mirthless, Urich said quietly, "Zar."

"But that's your father!"

"Yes. You were meant to be my father's bride. He won't forgive my betrayal of him, the son promising to deliver the keys to his kingdom—only to dangle them just within his reach before taking what was his for myself. Zar doesn't have the ability to love, but after this he may find himself quite capable of hatred."

"But no father, not even yours, could sentence his own son to death—could he?" When Urich said nothing, she shook him as if she could shake some sense into his father and him both. "If that's the kind of creature he is, then you have to stay here. Stay here with me. We'll hide if have to, we'll—"

"We'll do nothing of the kind," he countered firmly. "Eva, they could retrieve us easier than you can program one of your holograms."

"I'm not going to let you go there alone." She clung to him, clearly determined to hold on for the ride he was preparing for. "We'll face them together. I'll tell them I seduced you and we fell in love and—"

"And they won't understand a word you say. All they'll hear is gibberish that defies their comprehension." He held her face in his hands as all that she had taught him about love and humanity welled up with a poignant intensity.

A tear—he could feel one, then two—gather in the corners of his eyes, then roll down his cheeks.

"You were right, Eva. Love hurts. It hurts so sweet and deep that I want to cry... with joy."

And then he kissed her with all the joy she'd brought to his soul, all the hunger that not even a lifetime together could appease. Deeper and deeper he kissed her, taking her down in a flood of sensation, filling her thoughts with his silent whisper.

I love you, Eva. Love yourself enough for us both and never forget that you can be all that you dare dream to be. Sleep with the lioness and call to her for courage and wisdom and comfort. She'll always be there, for she's the very core of you. Dream now ... sweet, deep dreams....

As she succumbed to a heavy slumber, Urich cradled her to him. For a time, he held her, just held her.

Time. No amount of shifting its fickle composition could erase the kiss of the beast. He could, and should, implant a false memory of an accident to explain his mark, but what harm was there in allowing Eva to ponder the mysterious?

"Admit it," he muttered harshly to himself, "you're selfish enough to hope it stirs some fragment of memory, that deep down she'll remember you like a lover from a past life."

Or a future life yet to come. That much he could hope for: that in another life the stars would be aligned in their favor rather than crossed.

But for now, he had to go over to the other side of the envelope; do what he could to ensure Eva's safety. And if he failed? They'd still want her willing and he nixed that with a mental command for her to resist the overtures of strangers, even if the form they took was that of a hologram.

The one she had initially taken him for would appear on cue—he'd see to that momentarily. But first ...

A last, lingering kiss to her neck. Forcing himself to let her go, to leave this marvelous world he was homesick for already, Urich streaked toward his fate as he returned her to the moment just before they met.

Like a dot beneath a microscope, he saw her in the illuminated foliage, heard her call, "Companion!"

Companion that he was and she would never meet, he protected her from the heartache his death would surely bring.

He made it as though he had never existed.

20

"HEY, EVA, WHAT'RE YOU doing holed up in your office while the rest of us are celebrating? C'mon, join the party."

"Sorry, Ethan, but I—I . . ." she rubbed at her temples. "Something's missing." Or *someone?* "The experiment failed on some level."

"Take a reality check! Eva, the experiment was a phenomenal success. The hologram showed up on cue and simulated a human interaction. What else could you want? Besides matter conversion, we're there!"

But *he* wasn't. Only . . . who was "he"? She had no idea; all Eva knew was that she'd kept staring at the hologram and thinking it looked all wrong. And as for its verbal and emotional responses, they'd been artificial, stilted; had left her feeling hollow, certain that something of indefinable magnitude was missing.

Since she couldn't make a case for what she didn't understand herself, and since she didn't want to rain on Ethan's parade, Eva made her excuses.

"I'll join you later. I'm not feeling quite right."

"Are you sick?" he asked with concern.

"No, I just feel really strange. Not quite disoriented, but . . ." If she explained it to Ethan, maybe she could figure it out herself. "It's like I'm caught in a lucid dream. And in it, I could leap over this building in a single bound, except I can't because I've been cut off at the knees."

"Huh?"

"I know it doesn't make any sense, but I feel invincible, capable of anything, only I know that I'm not and—" *Belief is the key.* "And I keep hearing this voice in my head. This wonderful, incredible voice. It's like nothing I've ever heard before, but it seems so close, so familiar."

"Get a grip, Eva." Shutting the door, Ethan approached her desk, oddly hesitant in his stride. "Strange, but you kind of look different. A little . . . wild and ferocious?"

She sensed something like a scratching within, something that should be scaring the hell out of her instead of imparting this transcendent calm. More than calm, it was awesome, making her feel like she was regal and bold and, yes, ferocious. Like a creature of courage and untamed desires.

Untamed desires? Now she knew she was losing it.

"Hey." Ethan was snapping his fingers. "You okay?"

She was losing it, but never had she felt so centered, so without the fear she should be up to her eyeballs in. "Fear eradicates power." She whispered the words that seemed to come from a great distance within, carried on the echo of that marvelous, comforting voice. "Belief accesses it."

"Did something happen in the chamber that messed with your head?" Ethan demanded with enough alarm for them both as he put a palm to her forehead. "No fever, but—" Leaning in, he squinted at her neck. "What's this on your neck, Eva?"

Touching it, she felt the rise of two half-moon shapes, their texture similar to scars. Scars that she could swear were pulsing, giving off a glowing sensation that spread through her fingertips.

Ethan pulled at her wrist. "It looks like a bite. But not a human bite." His frown deepened. "You didn't have that before the experiment. What the hell happened in there?"

"I . . . something. Yes, something happened. But I—I can't remember." Grabbing his hand, she noticed he jumped as if her fingertips carried an electrical jolt. "Something happened, Ethan, but I don't know what. What happened to me?"

"The hell if I know, but one thing's for sure—this is getting too creepy. Maybe we should put off calling our funders with the news. We need to find out more before we take this public. Putting out a mind-blowing invention is one thing, but I don't want to be responsible for sending anyone into the Twilight Zone."

"Agreed," she said vaguely. She might have been amazed that they were finally in synch on the ethics end of their collaboration, but her mind was elsewhere, combing for a thread that would lead her to the source of this mystery.

"Why don't you let me drive you home? I'm worried about you, Eva. More than worried. I . . . I care about you."

"I know you do." Yes, Ethan did care about her, and the way he cared wasn't at all professional. *How did she know that?* And how did she know, know in her gut that her own heart could never be Ethan's because it belonged to another? But . . . who? There was no "other," and yet she heard herself say, "I'm sorry, Ethan, but you care in a way that I can't. There's someone else."

"Who?" he demanded. When she shrugged—the best answer she had—he smacked her desk. "Damn. And here I thought you were too busy at work to eke out the time for a date. Guess you found it anyway, huh?"

"Anything's possible," she reflected, saying what she'd heard before . . . somewhere. "Anything you can imagine, if you believe strongly enough, is within your ability to reach."

"Oh, yeah? Are you telling me if I imagine long enough that you're nuts about me, it's gonna happen? Much as I wish it was true, there're some things that a mind can't work over matter, and scoring with you is one of 'em."

"What did you say?" she asked, coming out of her chair.

"Down, girl. No need to get pissed because scoring with you is my favorite fantasy. There, the cat's out of the bag, and too bad for me I'll never get closer than—"

"No, not the scoring part. What you said about—about mind over matter."

"What about it?"

Indeed, what about it? Eva grabbed her purse, but she didn't bother to lock her desk since Ethan would probably pick it anyway. *What?* Where did that come from? At the door, she said, "You've been snooping in my desk, haven't you?"

His expression sheepish, Ethan confessed, "Only to play with some of your girl stuff. Sorry, Eva, I won't do that anymore. Especially now that I know there's someone else. Lucky bastard, I'd like to meet this guy."

"You—" *already have.* She took a deep breath, needing some fresh air. "Later, Ethan. I'm going home."

Eva was almost there when she stomped on the brake in front of an outdoor café. A woman at one of the tables sparked recognition that was too insistent not to investigate.

Pulling into the closest parking spot, Eva approached the woman, who looked up at her quizzically.

"Excuse me," Eva said. "We've met before, haven't we?"

"No."

"But I know you. You're—you're . . . Would you mind telling me your name?"

The woman minded, judging from her pause. "Justine."

"Justine . . . Justine . . ." Eva repeated. "You're wrong. We have met before," she insisted.

"Look, I don't know you, but if you've got a problem—"

"You—you like older men."

"Who doesn't, especially if they're rich? Oh, waiter—"

"And you drink . . . fuzzy navels?"

"Yeah. Waiter, could you come over here? This woman—"

Eva didn't stick around for the waiter to toss her out. Leaving her car behind, she walked in a daze, feeling trapped in a time warp, a déjà-vu loop-de-loop. Ethan had told her to get a grip. Justine had thought she was pushing the envelope of sanity. *The envelope.* Envelope, envelope. *What envelope?*

Nearing her neighborhood video store, Eva saw a large, tall man with waist-length black hair go inside. Her heart raced faster than her feet as she went after him. He was reaching for a movie when she latched onto his arm with the same impulsive instinct that had her calling him by name.

"Urich," she said, wondering just who Urich could be.

"Excuse me?" The man's pale blue eyes regarded her with interest.

"I . . . I'm sorry, but I thought you were someone else."

He glanced at her grip on his arm and she quickly let go, edging away while she continued to stare at him in confusion. "His eyes are green," she muttered. "Very green and like a glass you can see forever in. A—a looking glass. And—and his features are exotic, different from yours, and . . . and . . ."

"Lady, you okay?"

Backing into a display, she heard it overturn, saw the man coming over, picking it up while she stood there with the walls pressing in. She had to get out, get away from the clerk anxiously asking if she needed some kind of help.

The clerk. She triggered the flash of a vision: Urich with a load of videos. The clerk devouring him like the eye candy he was. *The clerk had seen him.*

"There's a man who comes here with me and he's about the size of this man, but he's darker and his hair is thicker and— Have you seen him? Have you seen Urich? I have to find him, but I don't know who—" *he is.* "Where he is."

Although she caught herself, the clerk and the man who bore a slight resemblance to Urich exchanged uneasy glances.

Eva suddenly realized they thought she must be a schizo on the loose who belonged in a straitjacket. And just maybe she did! But she did have enough screws intact to say, "Have a nice day," then escape the store.

The minute Eva reached home, she went straight for the brandy—only to slosh more on the counter than she was able to land in the snifter. In her mind's eye she saw an elegant, manly finger point to the bottle and alter the liquid's direction as that voice again teased her inner ear. *The laws of gravity are not as indelible as you think.*

"Who are you?" she demanded. Taking the bottle with her, she went from room to room, crying, "Where are you? Damn, what are you doing to me?"

In her bedroom, she stopped. Everything was the same, but it wasn't the same at all. It was too empty in here and yet it seemed full of memories she couldn't remember.

The dipping sun cast a rosy blush on the walls that were whispering secrets she couldn't catch. *I hunger.... Come, Beauty.... Kiss ... your Beast....*

"Stop this!" she begged, pounding the wall until she fell to the floor in a messy, hysterical heap of racking sobs. The bottle rolled from her numb hand as she crumpled inside, feeling an agony of loss, only God knowing what it was, but it was there and growing, tearing her apart as surely as someone called Urich was the cause.

When her sobbing ended, she lay there in the dark, her hair soaking in a pool of tears and brandy. Turning her lips to the wood planking, she sipped at the drink she'd yet to consume. She could have been a dog, was her thought, if she put her tongue to lapping. Lord, what was she doing here? Drinking like an animal and mewling like a wounded cat—

Animal? A cat? No, not exactly a cat, but a ... lioness.

"Yeah, right, Eva," she said with a shrill laugh. "You're hearing voices, imagining things that didn't happen and people who don't exist. You are going to take a bath. Then you are going to bed. And when you wake up in the morning, if you don't have your act together, you will call a shrink. Get it? Got it. Good."

Pulling herself up, she stripped off her clothes and wiped the floor with them. Then she took her bath and went to bed. But then came his voice, whispering, *I love you, Eva. Love yourself.... You can be all that you dare dream to be....*

Eva switched on the radio, turned it up loud enough to clean her ears out and fill her head with the last words she needed to hear from the Moody Blues or anyone else puzzling where reality ended and illusion began.

THERE WAS NO NEED for a holding cell. Raven glanced at Urich as they took their places behind Zar, who headed the processional that would lead to their certain end.

It was a foregone conclusion: self-inflicted death. Urich would be given the blade first; Urich's blood still fresh on it, his coconspirator in this matter of the heart would then turn it on himself and end his existence as well.

Zar had been so incensed by the news, Raven had thought them lucky to even get a hearing. But he'd taken a perverse pleasure in seeing Zar ready to do murder, as apparently had Urich, who had taunted his father to do it.

That's when it had occurred him that while his own honor would demand he accept his sentence, Urich could refuse. Now *that* would put some life into this stale piece of the universe, which could use a kick in its logically collective butt!

Why, he hadn't felt this alive in a millenium himself. Less than a day on Earth and he would trade whatever life he had remaining for another—but there wasn't much remaining, even if by some miracle he was spared. He was old but Urich was young and not deserving this at all.

Urich, who had made him remember what it was like to be so enraptured with a female that he threw reason to the wind. A female worth dying for; one who could make him lust, make him love, make him infinitely more than the sum of his parts.

All this Raven thought upon as the members took their designated places while he and Urich, the accused, stood at the far end of the vast table, a slab of silver that lacked any warmth. Zar had even less as he took his position at the head where he piously recounted the charges against them.

"Conspiracy. Breaking the supreme laws of logic. Adulterating the sacred ritual to defile the womb of conception. Treason by desertion of service, honor and duty." Done with his accusations, Zar demanded, "What say you to these atrocities committed against your ruler, your people?"

Turning to Urich, Raven embraced him, thus inciting the murmurs of incredulity their list of crimes hadn't summoned.

Loud enough for them all to hear, Raven announced, "I say Urich is a superior being that all of us could learn greatly from. I give him my eternal gratitude for reminding me that the worst atrocity is to live without love—and to live without it, a fate worse than death."

STANDING ON THE BALCONY, Eva stared up at the starry night. Filtering from her room was the music that had led her outside with nothing on but a thin, white cotton gown.

It was chilly out but it had nothing on the chill gripping her within. "Nights in White Satin" had prompted stunning, vivid images of intimacy shared on her bed with a man whose face and form had crystallized in her mind.

"Question" had provoked more questions than she already had. But there were answers to be found in "The Voice," which spoke of dreams, the future, the past. . . .

Urich. She could hear his voice, feel him like an infinite echo in her heart, her mind; so real and so pure that she knew, *knew* that he had been no more a dream than she was now, asking herself along with the Moody Blues, "Isn't Life Strange?"

How strange to remember falling into his looking-glass gaze and seeing "forever" in his eyes, only for time to naysay that memory, as unshakable as it was sweet.

Where had their time together gone? Memories that were poignant, fantastical, were surfacing. But there were holes, big gaping holes she was desperate to fill; and how desperate she was to understand how she could have memories that sprang from an empty pocket of time. It was as if it had been swallowed with the totality of quicksand.

Quicksand? Swallowing, erasing . . . *yes.* Urich had phenomenal abilities, she remembered that. But how could any man reverse time? Only. . . *he wasn't a man!* He came from— from . . . where?

Catching at the escalating images she frantically tried to piece together, Eva's eyes probed the night sky. He was out there, somewhere in another world, gone from this one where she'd searched without knowing what she was looking for.

And now she knew.

She had to find him. *Had to.* It was coming back to her now, quickly, except . . . why had he gone? Anxiety gnawed at her until it became a dread certainty that something terrible had happened to break them apart. But they were supposed to be together, always, mates for life. He had given her—

Eva cupped her neck. *The kiss of the beast.* An eternal kiss that not even time with its fickle composition could erase. A claim so indelible that they were still locked, bonded with memories that refused to yield to Urich's tampering.

A memory of him bowing to her with flowers, kissing her hand as if she were a queen of the universe, coincided with the announcer's apt conclusion: "And now, ending our tribute to the Moody Blues, 'For My Lady.'"

With that, Eva had the last elusive piece to the puzzle of Urich's departure. The song was about a man who so loved a woman that he would give up his life for her—freely, completely.

Clutching at her neck, struggling for breath, she wheezed, "My God, oh, my God, he's—"

She had to find him, save him, die with him—anything but stay here and know Urich was dead while she died her own slow death, mourning his loss.

"That's it for now. This is Casey Kasem and until next time, remember to keep your feet on the ground and keep reaching for the stars!"

Her gaze fixed on the North Star, Eva chanted Urich's name like a mantra while holding fast to all that he had taught her and she did believe. Yes, belief was the key. She believed in herself and knew that anything she could imagine having was within her ability to reach.

Eva imagined a telepathic wire running from her to him, just past the envelope and into the Black Hole.

And then she reached for the stars.

21

ZAR PROFFERED the death blade with a curt bow. Urich defiantly crossed his arms, knowing his life was the only bargaining chip he had and it was time to go for broke.

"Do it," he challenged. "Go ahead, Zar, kill your treasonous hybrid of a son. I can read your thoughts and you want to stab me in the heart that's responsible for this whole distasteful and painfully embarrassing mess."

"You're embarrassing yourself," Zar snapped. "After insulting us all and debasing yourself with that sentimental tripe you called a justifiable defense, the least you can do is execute your last order with some dignity."

"You dare to speak to me about dignity?" he scoffed. "You, Zar, are a coward. Now, go ahead and stab all you like. No one could possibly blame you. And I'm sure it would be the most emotionally rich experience of your sad excuse for an existence. My own I owe to you, but nothing else. No excuses, no apologies. If you feel that I owe you the life you regret ever giving me, then take it."

Zar gripped the hilt and raised the blade. Urich met his livid glare steadily. And smiled.

They both knew that to do murder was to break a law higher than any of those Urich himself had broken. And how sweet it was to provoke Zar to a crime of passion, make him walk in the other man's shoes, as Earthlings would say.

Suddenly Urich's smile wavered. He perceived Zar's sly retaliation just before he turned to Raven.

"Urich's always admired you more than any other. Show him how to die with honor and we'll honor your remains with respect and gratitude for this final act of service."

Raven hesitated only briefly before slowly reaching for the means to restoring his honor, while his mind spoke a plea that Urich refuse to follow the order his elder was compelled to obey.

"Wait." Urich gripped Raven's wrist within an inch of the hilt. "Even if Raven slays himself first, I won't take the blade. And I'm the one whose blood you really want—it just depends on how badly you want it."

Zar raised an eyebrow. "You wish to strike a bargain?"

"A fair and logical exchange. First, my life for his." Although the ruler had the final vote, Zar glanced at the assembly.

Much as Urich hated to admit it, especially now, his father was a just ruler, wholly devoted to his people. All present pressed forefinger to temple, signing their agreement.

"Very well. What else?"

"Leave Eva alone."

"What!"

"You heard me. Leave her alone and search for another who'd bear our progeny willingly. Eva will resist you. And I'll resist my sentence unless you agree, and so long as I'm alive, you can't have her anyway. This leaves you with the option of killing me yourself—an offer you already refused—or promising to leave her untouched. Whether I die or not, you can't claim her. These are my terms, nonnegotiable. Again I ask you, how badly do you want my blood?"

A grudging respect flickered in Zar's eyes for the mental strategy even he could appreciate.

As did the Tribunal, to whom he turned for the ultimate decision. One by one they opened their palms. A sign of returning the decision to Zar.

Urich was certain it pleased Zar—his authority remaining unquestioned, his judgment upheld. He was emerging unscathed, getting his revenge without soiling his reputation or the blade-wielding hand he extended to the son he had never loved.

Without a qualm, Urich gripped the hilt; then placed the razor-point tip to his steady heartbeat.

"A final request," he said calmly. "Allow Raven to return to Earth if he so desires."

"Granted. Have you any last words?"

There really were none. He'd driven a hard bargain and won each and every demand placed.

"Farewell, Raven." Raising the blade to plunge, he issued his parting charge. "Have enough fun for us both."

His gaze on the gleaming tip, Urich filled his mind with thoughts of Eva and was about to slice down when her voice shattered the silence, screaming, *"Stop! Stop!"*

Urich stopped in mid-plunge, stunned by the sight of Eva racing at lightning speed over the table's surface, a ripple of shocked gasps following in her wake.

The gasps were almost as amazing as seeing Eva fly like an avenging angel in the see-through gown she raised to her thighs to better run while she shrieked, "Put it down, Urich! Damn, did you hear me? *Put it Down!*"

Down she came from the table, leaping over the end. Urich was too dumbfounded to move. Only his heart was in motion—rising, beating too fast, reaching out for the woman who seized his hands and the blade they held.

He caught her to him in a fierce embrace. "Eva, Eva," he said over the rampant murmurings. "What are you doing here? How did you—"

"We'll hash it out later," she briskly informed him. Breaking away, she waved the blade at the assembly. "Right now,

I have a score to settle and anybody that's not ready for a nasty earful had better clear out."

All save one leaned eagerly forward.

Zar stepped back, folded his arms. "Who do you think you are to intrude where you have not been sanctioned to come?"

Pointing the shiny tip at his nose, Eva commanded herself not to swipe off its superior tilt but to say, cool as ice, "I'm Eva Campbell and I want to know just who do you think you are to sanction a kangaroo court like this? Don't tell me. You must be Zar. If you were younger and had something called a heart, I might even mistake you for Urich." Lowering the weapon to Zar's chest, she mused, "I wonder if I put this to a worthy use if I'd even find one."

"Are you mad?" he asked, sounding truly curious.

"Oh, yeah, I'm mad, all right. Madder than hell, to be exact. In fact, I am so damn mad right now, you'd be real smart to explain to me where you get off expecting your son to kill himself because we fell in love and shared our bodies to express what we felt."

"Our laws are not yours," he said succinctly, as if that was explanation and justification aplenty. Studying her, he observed, "Your body is pleasing to look upon." From the ranks came a rousing agreement that made Eva wish she'd come wearing a chastity belt. "Yes, quite pleasing. How unfortunate that I vowed not to touch you in exchange for Urich answering to his crimes."

"Falling in love is not a crime! Not loving your son more than your twisted sense of justice—*that's* a crime!" Her grip tightened on the hilt and Eva silently wondered if she was capable of killing. She'd never thought so before, but just as a lioness would kill to protect her young, as a mother would to save her loved ones, Eva knew she wouldn't hesitate to do the same. "If anyone deserves to die, Zar, it's you."

"I am not on trial, therefore your judgment bears no consideration." Just like that, he dismissed her with an authoritative command. "Give Urich the blade. His trial is over and he's accepted his executioner's duty. Our agreement is sealed and you've delayed our proceedings long enough."

Eva gaped at Zar. Didn't he have ears to hear? And then she remembered Urich saying that they wouldn't understand a word she said. True enough, she could have been speaking a foreign language for all that Zar had comprehended.

"Eva," Urich said firmly, "the deal is struck. You can't change what's already been ordained. Kiss me once, then you have to go." In disbelief, she watched his lips descend, felt them move over hers, imparting all that he was, all that he felt and thought, with a tender passion. But when his fingers slipped over hers and he tried to claim the knife, Eva jerked away and put the edge to her jugular.

"No. I'll kill myself before I'll let you have this." Swiftly, she moved from his reach, positioned herself where all could see her. "If it's blood you want, I'll give mine."

"Eva, enough," Urich chastised. "Give me that. Raven, prepare to take her home."

"Certainly."

Raven advanced and she threatened, "Come any closer, and this jig's over. I want to strike a new deal. *My* deal. Forget Urich's."

"Dr. Campbell," Zar said reasonably, "your blood is not wanted, nor is it needed. You bear no guilt and there is no need for you to suffer. Or to strike another deal."

"A better deal. One that'll get you what you want and me what I want."

"I'm intrigued. Go on."

"You're not going on anywhere but home," Urich informed her, slowly closing in.

"This is between me and your father." Fearing that Urich would zap her home or seize the only leverage she had, Eva appealed to her only hope—ironically, Zar. "I want an hour alone. One-on-one, just you and me, Zar."

Before Urich could protest, Raven intervened. "She is affected by this as well, Urich. Let Eva have the audience she desires. It's the right thing to do."

Fingertips to temples, the Tribunal gave their affirmative concurrence.

"Yes," Zar agreed. "It is just."

Urich's glare was accusing. "Have it your way, Eva. Just don't make me further regret that you came here."

His ungracious acquiescence stung, but Eva knew he was smarting even more. She had publicly overruled her mate in front of his peers, and in this male-dominated society, that was quite a blow. Lord, but they needed some women to straighten them up and turn them around.

"Come, Dr. Campbell." Although Zar didn't offer his arm, she took it anyway.

He stiffened at her touch, but Eva held on. It was the first step of the plan she snuffed from her mind. If Urich got a whiff of her intentions, God only knew what he would do. For sure he'd do more than all the snarling he was doing now.

It lanced her ears as they exited, and she knew Urich was this close to lunging, asserting his primal claim.

Only after they reached a private room did Eva breathe a sigh of relief.

"I, too, am surprised he was able to restrain himself," Zar commented as he removed her grip—regretfully, she thought. "Such contact of a female mate can incite a violent reaction in the male. For all Urich's misguided behavior, it seems that he did acquire some discipline over his instincts during his stay on Earth."

Zar motioned her to a streamlined metal chair, which she disdained for what passed as a couch. Patting the space beside her, she invited, "Sit with me."

"So, Urich was correct in saying that you humans like physical proximity." Seating himself at the far end, Zar shifted uncomfortably when she scooted close beside him. "Please, Dr. Campbell, this really isn't—"

"Call me Eva. We don't have much time, so let's drop the formalities and get down to business."

"Ah...yes, the deal." He jerked when she ran a finger from his knee to his thigh, sucked in his breath as she began to lightly stroke. "What do you think you're—"

"This is the deal. You want babies. I can give them to you. Finding someone else means you'll have to start from scratch. I'm here and I'm willing to get to it right now."

"Dr. Camp—"

"Eva," she whispered seductively into his ear.

"E-Eva. You must stop this. It-it's not acceptable."

"Who cares? Don't you want your race to continue?"

"Of course, but . . ." he groaned at her nip to his earlobe.

"I can help you, Zar. Spare Urich and I'll give you babies. But you'll have to let me raise them, give them the emotional values of my people. We can work something out with logistics—divvy up the time between our two worlds."

"How—how can you profess this thing called love to my son and betray him with your hands on me like this?"

"Only love could drive anyone to a desperate act. That's what this is, Zar. I'll do anything to save him, even if it means selling my soul and bartering my body for a man who'll never forgive me for it." The stakes so high she was queasy, Eva courted Zar's capitulation and forced herself to lightly brush his crotch—one that surely hadn't been touched in an eon, judging from his strangled groan and the rise of his hips, as she quickly returned her palm to his knee. "Take the deal,

Zar," she purred over the heaving of her stomach. "Take it, take me, and let him go."

"But he would rather die."

"Why should you care?" she asked, blowing the question into his ear.

"I—I don't know. But this not only goes against our code of honor, it feels wrong."

"*Feels*," she repeated, inching her hand higher, not giving a damn about his honor or hers, just desperate, beyond desperate to cinch her win. "See? You can feel, after all. Feel me, Zar," she murmured, leading his hand near her breast. "Feel what it's like to want something . . . someone so much that even if you know it's wrong, you can't help yourself."

"Help me," he begged. "Remove my hand. I can't. I—I've never touched anything like this."

"Urich tried to resist me, too, but he didn't stand a chance. So, how does it feel, Zar? How does it feel to be in the position he was in?"

"It . . . it's horrible. Wonderful."

"Oh, yes, it is," she assured him. And then she beseeched him, "If you can understand what he went through, can't you show him some mercy?"

"You're torturing me," he said raggedly. "Why are you doing this?"

"Because our time's running out and you have to make a decision." When his reply was a frantic clutch at her breast, Eva steeled herself to further compromise them both. "Take it out, see what you're touching."

With a savage swipe, he rent the bodice of her gown. But how reverent was his awestruck gaze, the trembling of his hand, as he lifted a single breast.

"You want to claim it, claim me."

"Yes, yes," he managed between groans.

"And you'll accept the better deal, right?"

His gaze was so devouringly needful, she was torn between pity for his starved senses and abject terror that her master plan was about to blow up in her face.

"Yes, anything. I accept anything for this." With a deep, yearning growl he bent to taste what he held.

Before he could take a single lick, Eva sprang from the couch and lifted her gown almost to her thighs.

"What—what are you doing?" he sputtered.

"Keeping my end of the bargain. I'm naked under my gown, so I'm ready. Pull down your pants and let's just do it." His jaw dropped and she demanded, "C'mon, what're you waiting for? Put your penis in my vagina, do what it takes to ejaculate, and we're done." Her deliberately clinical summation got the right reaction. Zar flushed as he covered his straining crotch with folded hands.

"I'm waiting," she taunted. "So is the Tribunal. And *Urich*. Considering you want to claim his mate, he might be a little upset."

"You tricked me!"

Oh, but she had, and Zar didn't know the half of it yet. "I just beat you at your own game. Now, about our deal—"

"There is no deal."

"Oh, yeah? With my own two ears I heard you say, and I quote: 'Yes, anything. I accept anything for this.' End quote. Now, according to you guys, once a deal is struck, you can't change what's already been ordained. You did, however, unordain Urich's deal in exchange for mine. Far be it from me to go back on my word—the deal *we* agreed to still stands. Unless you unordain this one, too."

Zar shook his head in bewilderment. "How could I have come so close to betraying my people? Urich could have had me emasculated and then there would be no hope for us at all."

"He still could," she argued, holding on to her hard line despite her sympathy for the jerk. But maybe, just maybe he wouldn't be such a jerk after this. Eva gestured to her bodice. "If I go back in there like this, he'll want to attack you and nobody would stop him. Your laws, Zar, could use some flexibility. Not to mention a little less logic and a lot more human empathy."

Zar considered that, and then he nodded. Once. "You make a good case, but we are not like your kind."

"You're like us enough to let something besides your brain do your thinking." Eva was gratified to see him blush. "You know, Zar, I think there's hope for you yet."

"Not if you return in the gown I tore. My deepest apologies for that . . . Eva."

He could get turned on. He could be angry, even blush and say he was sorry. Definitely there was hope.

"I could be persuaded to change."

"How?" he asked, coming out his seat and quickly jerking her bodice together. More quickly still, he clasped his hands behind his back.

Eva pinched his cheek. And smiled. Conspiratorially.

"Forget the other two, I'm gonna make you a deal you can't refuse. A honey of a deal, Zar. You're gonna *love* it."

22

WHERE WERE THEY? Urich wondered in the ferocious silence he had kept. He couldn't track them in movement or thought, his own mind a maelstrom of turbulent emotion.

If Zar touched her, even once, he'd carve out Zar's crotch before he put the blade to himself. That's exactly what he'd do—wasn't it? He'd have every right. But then again, would it be fair for his race to become extinct so he could 'have his pound of flesh,' as Eva had once put it?

Damn her, anyway. She made him see things from that convoluted human perspective of hers. And even if by some miracle she skewed Zar's perspective as well, the woman would be the death of him yet.

He should have been dead by now. But then came Eva, roaring like the lioness she was, cutting her teeth on his heart and his pride, while every male in their midst licked their lips as they savored the sight of *his* mate.

Even now, all eyes were on the spot where she had exited. And even now, as she and Zar made a regal entrance together, Eva dressed in Deducian attire—much too clingy, it left nothing to the imagination, or rather, too much—the assembly rose in expectation, then bowed to her as if she were the queen of their universe, wrapped in a wet dream.

Urich forced himself not to stalk up to the impossibly smiling Zar and wrench Eva's hand from his arm. She was smiling, too—a grin that was between a glow and a gloat.

Her eyes, shining and bright, caught his. Eva winked.

Before he could ponder what in the world she had managed to pull off, Zar bypassed his exalted end of the table and directed their sweeping pace to where Urich stood, waiting in amazement. Amazement on top of amazement, Zar extended his hand and said, "She is yours. You are free. Shake on it?"

Urich was about to grip the hand Zar offered, but stopped short. "I'll hear the deal first."

"As she said, she gets what she wants, and I get what I want. It's a . . . honey of a deal? A deal I couldn't refuse. I agreed, certain the Tribunal would be thrilled as well with what Eva so generously offered."

Eva? Thrilled? Urich wasn't sure which term alarmed him the most. "You've never been thrilled a day in your life. And as for your familiar reference to my mate, I'm not overly thrilled with that."

"But she is going to be my daughter-in-law. Aren't you, my dear?"

"Absolutely," Eva confirmed. "After we go through some formalities here to do it up right, Zar wants to come with us to Vegas to give the bride away. And Raven, you'll stand up as a witness both places, won't you?"

"Of—of—but, of course. I would be honored."

Eva pecked his cheek, then turned her gaze to Urich. She sent him love and laughter as softly she said, "Shake your father's hand, Urich. It's the right thing to do."

His trust in Eva implicit, he took Zar's offering.

"I was wrong," Zar said. "Forgive me for my crimes against you and your woman, Urich."

A crime against Eva? "What happened in there?"

Eva and Zar exchanged a secretive glance.

"Quite simply, she made me understand the virtues of a woman's wiles, the merits of empathy, the rare treasure to be had in being loved as deeply as she does you." With an eloquent bow to Eva he added, "*And* the benefits of compromise."

23

"SHE'S PERFECT FOR our purposes, Urich."

"Indeed, Raven, I do believe we have another gem to add to our celestial crown." Urich's gaze sharpened on the latest lady of adventure he'd put his mind to seeking out.

"Would you stop that!" Eva pinched his thigh beneath the pub table. "For heaven's sake, Urich, how many more woman do you need? The Tribunal's starting to look like a harem, and Zar has enough catfights to make me wonder why he's taking his sweet time deciding which one he wants for a mate."

"He's waiting to fall in love and wants just the right one to laugh and argue and get beastly with. After all, once he picks, she's it and his days of fawning females are done."

Even as he said it, Urich could hardly believe he was actually speaking up for his father. But Zar had changed, as they all had. Humanity was proving highly contagious, but it seemed everyone in Deducia was eager to catch the germs. And as for love, what a deliciously rampant plague it had started.

"Besides, Eva, it was your idea," he proudly reminded. "And what a marvelous idea it was."

She blew on her knuckles and shined them on her shirt. "I did okay. But to tell the truth, I didn't expect so many volunteers. Or virtually all of them wanting to stay."

"Why should this surprise you?" Raven asked, joining in. "They're revered by our males and even those who believe themselves unattractive are gazed at in wonderment of their beauty by what they consider to be the 'hunks of the universe.' Besides that, no matter how badly they cook, their dishes are raved over. And to top it all off, any mate they take will never, ever stray."

"Here, here," Eva said, raising her beer in salute.

Three amber longnecks clinked. Sipping his, Raven went on. "Anyway, it seems enough incentive to stay rather than return to their previous lives, thinking they've suffered some temporary amnesia. Then again, they could keep their memories along with their mates and live as the two of you do. But none seem so inclined—unless we're displaced—but at least we could all survive here now that we've found our balance between logic and the illogical wisdom of women."

Urich laced his fingers with Eva's and squeezed. They both knew that Raven had left out a sensitive detail: children—a contributing factor to Zar being in such demand. Those who had paired up knew it was a trade-off, a devoted mate in exchange for the children they could never have.

Not wanting to talk about it, Urich said, "Well, it's easier for them to stay without having family to grieve over their absence. So many orphans—I'm glad they seem to feel that they've found family among us and themselves."

"Me, too." Eva nuzzled closer to her husband, her lover, her companion for life. She had news—great wonderful news—and couldn't wait to tell him. With a kittenish lick of her lips, she whispered, "Let's go home. Tomorrow's our two-year anniversary, but I'd like to celebrate tonight."

He gave her a swift kiss, then insisted on paying the tab. Eva let him, knowing what pride he took in his Earth earnings. Big bucks, too. Urich gave new meaning to Psychic of the Stars. Quite a splash he'd made with his accuracy and unerringly transcendent advice. He gave it free to those he perceived were in need of some guidance, and stuck it to

Hollywood—which was a lot more impressed with him than he was with anything so "fleeting as fame and Jags," as he put it.

"We're calling it a night, Raven," he said. "As always, we'd be happy to have you stay with us."

"Actually, I need to get back. Darla's probably missing me and I know that I'm missing her." He sighed with delight. "Who would have thought that I'd feel like a boy again at my age? Oh, but I'm happy these days. And Eva, I am so happy for you. Congratulations again on the grand opening of your interactive amusement center. At Disneyland, right?"

"Right." Maybe she wasn't Tinker Bell, but she'd managed to sprinkle her share of fairy dust on others. It seemed that some had landed on Ethan, who was currently honeymooning in the Caribbean and up to his elbows in researching what she'd refused to learn from Urich. "We can check out the holodeck the next time you're here."

"It's a date. I don't suppose you'll have a matter converter incorporated by then."

"No way," she assured him. She was perfectly happy with things just the way they were. The holodeck was the newest craze, but nobody was going crazy or being controlled. It was an escape that lent some borrowed companionship to those who needed it and simple amusement to those who didn't. And good old free enterprise was preventing any power mongering of innocent people. The funders were selling patents like mad.

"Tell me, Eva, why is it that you don't want what's there for the taking?"

"Let's just say, Raven, that invention, like relationships and time, has to take its natural course. You know us humans, having to evolve at our own snail's pace while we play catchup with you guys."

They left Raven laughing heartily.

"It is pretty funny," she said as Urich drove in a brooding silence. "I mean, for anyone to become so highly evolved only to take a giant step back to get where they need to be going—with the help of lower life-forms, no less."

His own chuckle was strained.

Should she tell him? She should, but this news was too good to spill in a car.

"Why don't you zap us home?" she suggested. "Do your 'I Dream of Jeannie' trick."

"It's closer to 'Bewitched,'" he muttered dryly.

Sliding her hand up his thigh, she knew how to get her way. "Oh, honey, if you don't zap us home, I'm going to be a very naughty girl and you know what happened the last time I had my way with you in a car. Remember, the one you totaled?"

Seconds later, Eva was giggling on top of him in their bed. "Did you put the car in the garage?"

"It's in. Now you have to deal with my beastly bedroom manners." With a lusty growl, he nipped her neck. "Purr for me," he commanded like the sweet beast he was.

"Ur-r-rich," she did indeed purr. "Or should I call you, mmm, how about . . . Daddy?"

With a wave of his hand, a dozen candles leaped to life. His beloved face, all angles and dark shadows, was etched in pained lines as he said tightly, "Eva, if this is your idea of a joke, it isn't funny."

"I know. And if you'll notice, I'm not laughing."

His eyes searched hers and she could see forever in his gaze. Like Alice through The Looking Glass, she tripped through and saw a rainbow of shimmering hope.

"We've got the pot of gold, Urich. The adoption agency called today and we have our *babies* on the way. Twins. A boy and a girl. They're a year old and flying in from Korea."

"But I thought—" He blinked back the quick tears of emotion she joyfully gave in to for them both. "They said my background was too sketchy, my profession too unstable, that we hadn't been married long enough. How . . . Why?"

"You're asking me?" Eva laughed and cried while he swept her face with kisses. "Belief is the key," she reminded him. "And now, oh great companion, before Beauty summons her Beast, read my thoughts and say with me . . ."

From the limiting perimeters of *Why?* they reached for the *Why not?* of the mysterious. Embracing it as they did each other, they said in unison, "Mind over matter."

HARLEQUIN®
Temptation®

Secret Fantasies

Do you have a secret fantasy?

Desiree Dupree does. By day she's an investigative
journalist. But at night she lets her imagination heat
up and pens erotic love stories. Dark and brooding
Roman Falconer is playing a starring role in her
personal fantasies. Except something *scary* is going on
in New Orleans and Reece is the prime suspect. Look
for #562 *Private Passions*, JoAnn Ross's newest
Temptation in November.

Everybody has a secret fantasy. And you'll find
them all in Temptation's exciting miniseries,
Secret Fantasies. Throughout 1995, one book each
month focuses on the hero or heroine's innermost
romantic desires....

OFFICIAL RULES

PRIZE SURPRISE SWEEPSTAKES 3448

NO PURCHASE OR OBLIGATION NECESSARY

Three Harlequin Reader Service 1995 shipments will contain respectively, coupons for entry into three different prize drawings, one for a Panasonic 31" wide-screen TV, another for a 5-piece Wedgwood china service for eight and the third for a Sharp ViewCam camcorder. To enter any drawing using an Entry Coupon, simply complete and mail according to directions.

There is no obligation to continue using the Reader Service to enter and be eligible for any prize drawing. You may also enter any drawing by hand printing the words "Prize Surprise," your name and address on a 3"x5" card and the name of the prize you wish that entry to be considered for (i.e., Panasonic wide-screen TV, Wedgwood china or Sharp ViewCam). Send your 3"x5" entries via first-class mail (limit: one per envelope) to: Prize Surprise Sweepstakes 3448, c/o the prize you wish that entry to be considered for, P.O. Box 1315, Buffalo, NY 14269-1315, USA or P.O. Box 610, Fort Erie, Ontario L2A 5X3, Canada.

To be eligible for the Panasonic wide-screen TV, entries must be received by 6/30/95; for the Wedgwood china, 8/30/95; and for the Sharp ViewCam, 10/30/95.

Winners will be determined in random drawings conducted under the supervision of D.L. Blair, Inc., an independent judging organization whose decisions are final, from among all eligible entries received for that drawing. Approximate prize values are as follows: Panasonic wide-screen TV ($1,800); Wedgwood china ($840) and Sharp ViewCam ($2,000). Sweepstakes open to residents of the U.S. (except Puerto Rico) and Canada, 18 years of age or older. Employees and immediate family members of Harlequin Enterprises, Ltd., D.L. Blair, Inc., their affiliates, subsidiaries and all other agencies, entities and persons connected with the use, marketing or conduct of this sweepstakes are not eligible. Odds of winning a prize are dependent upon the number of eligible entries received for that drawing. Prize drawing and winner notification for each drawing will occur no later than 15 days after deadline for entry eligibility for that drawing. Limit: one prize to an individual, family or organization. All applicable laws and regulations apply. Sweepstakes offer void wherever prohibited by law. Any litigation within the province of Quebec respecting the conduct and awarding of the prizes in this sweepstakes must be submitted to the Regies des loteries et Courses du Quebec. In order to win a prize, residents of Canada will be required to correctly answer a time-limited arithmetical skill-testing question. Value of prizes are in U.S. currency.

Winners will be obligated to sign and return an Affidavit of Eligibility within 30 days of notification. In the event of noncompliance within this time period, prize may not be awarded. If any prize or prize notification is returned as undeliverable, that prize will not be awarded. By acceptance of a prize, winner consents to use of his/her name, photograph or other likeness for purposes of advertising, trade and promotion on behalf of Harlequin Enterprises, Ltd., without further compensation, unless prohibited by law.

For the names of prizewinners (available after 12/31/95), send a self-addressed, stamped envelope to: Prize Surprise Sweepstakes 3448 Winners, P.O. Box 4200, Blair, NE 68009.

RPZ KAL